THE A-TEAM II:
SMALL BUT DEADLY WARS

All four doors of the police cruiser opened
simultaneously, and uniformed officers stepped out, then
closed the doors in chilling unison. Bathed in the
bounding light of the rooftop beacon, they all stared
coldly at Ed Maloney. One of them took a few steps
forward, becoming a silhouette tinged with blue.

'Do you know how hard it is to prosecute a cop?'

'Cops?' Ed sneered, squinting to meet the eyes of all four
men. 'You have the nerve to call yourselves cops? You're
killers, that's what you are. Murderers; hit men killing
for money.'

'Forget about that appointment you have tomorrow
morning,' was the reply.

Maloney flinched slightly. He hadn't thought they'd
known about his meeting with the chief. If they'd found
out about that, what else were they on to? Did they
know he'd been trying to get in touch with outside help?
Did they know about the A-Team?

Also available

THE A-TEAM

THE A-TEAM II
SMALL BUT DEADLY WARS

A novel by Charles Heath

Based on the television series 'The A-Team'
Created by Frank Lupo & Stephan J. Cannell
Adapted from the episodes 'A Small and
Deadly War', written by Frank Lupo, and
'Black Day at Bad Rock', written by Patrick
Hansburgh

A TARGET BOOK

published by
the Paperback Division of
W. H. ALLEN & Co. Ltd

A Target Book
Published in 1984
by the Paperback Division of
W.H. Allen & Co. Ltd
A Howard and Wyndham Company
44 Hill Street, London W1X 8LB

Printed in Great Britain by
Hunt Barnard Printing Ltd., Aylesbury, Bucks.

ISBN 0 426 19713 5

PROLOGUE

The Los Angeles freeway system is a world unto itself. A world on wheels, composed of tarmac, steel, flesh and concrete, alive with the blur of restless activity, filled with cars hurtling toward a thousand destinations at speeds ranging from a turtle's pace to full-throttled haste. At any given hour, there are enough motorists rolling their way through LA's miles of asphalt to match the populations of some countries. And no two are the same. Maniacs, born-again Christians, haggard dogfood salesmen wrapping up a week of peddling Wonder Kibble – souls from all stations in life share the many lanes that course through this, one of the world's largest cities. It's no wonder that a television series based on the exploits of motorcops patrolling the rolling range of highway could run for years and never run short of fresh plots. The freeway breeds drama with the same inevitable certainty with which it breeds chuckholes and builds up a residue of retread shrapnel from speeding Mack trucks that shed the rubber from their hot and anguished wheels.

More often than not, the greatest drama seems to unfold along the less-trafficked stretches of roadway, as in the case of the cool spring evening when Ed Maloney was driving home on the Simi Freeway, which threaded its way between the foothills of the Santa Susanna Mountains and the suburban sprawl of the San Fernando Valley. Behind the wheel of his fender-creased Plymouth Fury, Maloney was a picture of worried concentration, dividing his attention between the road before him and the view behind, as afforded by a rear-view mirror that trailed a gold-chained pendant containing the small, framed picture of a smiling woman. He wasn't smiling back at the picture, though. The interior of the car was only a few degrees warmer than outside, but Maloney was sweating. Sweating the kind of sweat that comes from fear, the kind of sweat that rolls past the raised hairs on one's neck and then trails down the spine with an icy chill. Maloney had faced more than his share of danger over the years, and there were scars pocking his thick, ruddy flesh to prove it, but there were certain matters that no amount of sheer nerve could prepare one for. He thought for a fleeting moment that a drink might help matters, and he licked his dry lips at the image of a fresh-drawn beer down at Hannigan's Bar. Maybe he'd stop there on the way home, park himself on a stool and mull things over between sips.

'Yeah,' he muttered to himself, freeing one hand from the wheel and fidgeting with the radio, turning up the volume for more distraction. A country love song twanged over the dashboard speaker as he sped past the Topanga Canyon Boulevard turnoff, the last chance to dip into the San Fernando Valley. He was headed west, entering a quiet corridor of pavement, flanked by hills, that would soon lead him into Simi Valley, a bedroom community sprouting from the influx of commuters seeking affordable housing after being priced out of most other areas in LA. Simi was home for Maloney. It was where he felt almost safe. He didn't care if some people thought the place was dull. At least you could leave the house without feeling like you were taking your own life in your hands. Better bored than buried, Ed Maloney always said.

As he pulled his hand away from the radio, Ed let his fingers drop to the seat beside him. They landed crisply on a plain manilla envelope lying there, and the contact seemed to ease his mind somewhat. He even let himself hum along with the song on the radio for a few bars. Then a sneeze crept to the rim of his nostrils and tickled the bristly hairs nestled there. Maloney sniffed loudly, but he couldn't shake the sneeze, and it burst forth with a force that made the flesh on his face quiver. Tears came to his eyes, and by the time he'd blinked them away, the moment he'd been dreading all night was upon him.

In the rearview mirror, red lights spun into life atop the roof of a car following a few lengths behind the Plymouth. When Maloney reflexively eased down on the accelerator and begun to lunge forward, the other car picked up speed, drawing closer still as it sounded a quick, shrill blast of its siren.

'Damn,' Maloney cursed dryly through his chapped lips as he glanced down at his speedometer. He was still within the speed limit, and he was driving in the middle of his lane. They weren't trying to stop him for a traffic violation. He knew it was something more serious than that. A lot more serious.

Snapping off the radio, Maloney briefly considered flooring the pedal and trying to make a run for it. He had more than three hundred horses under his hood, and he knew how to make them race. He might be able to give the other car the slip, at least for a moment, but if they were expecting a chase, they'd catch up to him before he could reach the next exit. Better to face them and take his chances, he decided. After all, he could be mistaken about them. Maybe one of his tail-lights were out and nothing more.

'Fat chance,' he whispered, trying to keep his shoulders straight so those that behind him couldn't see that he was reaching for the manilla envelope and quickly stuffing it under his seat as he snapped on his turning signal and slowed down. Easing the Plymouth onto the shoulder, Maloney unzipped his jacket and bared the butt of a .38 revolver tucked into a leather shoulder holster. After undoing the snap that held the gun in place, he transferred it quickly into the pocket of his jacket. His palm was sweating, so he wiped it off on his knee as he brought his car to a halt on the gravel and watched the auto in the mirror do the same.

The traffic had thinned out considerably the past few miles. A few cars whisked by Maloney as he swung his door open and climbed out of the Plymouth, keeping one hand in his pocket. The dryness around his lips had spread throughout his mouth and down his throat. He felt as if he were choking. He was shaking slightly, too, caught up in the grip of fear. Staring into the headlights of the police cruiser, he fought back a mad urge to empty his gun into the pulsing bulbs to make them stop flashing in his face. His nerves were taut and it took all the will power he had left inside him to remain calm and await the inevitable confrontation.

All four doors of the police cruiser opened simultaneously, and uniformed officers stepped out, then closed the doors in chilling unison. Bathed in the bounding light of the rooftop beacon, they all stared coldly at Ed Maloney. One of them took a few steps forward, becoming a silhouette tinged with blue. When he spoke, his voice had a lifeless quality that carried through the night like a creaking of unoiled gears.

'Do you know how hard it is to prosecute a cop?'

Ed Maloney shifted alongside his car, feeling a faint spurt of courage shoot through him. They were here to talk. What a relief. He'd expected to already be lying facedown in his own blood by now, comforted only in the knowledge that he'd taken a few of them with him. But they just wanted to talk. There was a chance he would live through the night after all. The thought made him braver by the moment.

'Cops?' he sneered, squinting to meet the eyes of all four men. 'You have the nerve to call yourself cops? You're killers, that's what you are. Murderers; hit men killing for money.'

As his eyes accustomed themselves to the eerie light, Maloney began to pick out discerning features on the faces of those watching him. There was Collins, with his thick eyebrows and even thicker moustache. Freckles were splashed across the face of Meadows like drops of dried blood. Shaeffer bore deep scars on his right cheek, compliments of a whore with long nails and a short temper. And Stark, out front, doing the talking, wearing that smug grin he always wore. God, did he hate the four of them. The inside of his index finger softly stroked the curved metal of the .38's trigger. If he didn't have a family to live for, he was sure he'd start firing any second at them. He could see that they all had their hands on their own service revolvers, but he figured he could nail at least Stark and Shaeffer before either of the others could get off a shot at him. If anybody started to pull their gun from their holsters, he wouldn't have a choice but to let loose.

'Forget about that appointment you have with Chief Metcalf tomorrow morning,' Stark told him. His voice was almost friendly now, the way a wolf almost looks like a sheep when it dresses in wool.

Maloney flinched slightly. Stark's warning shaved the edge off his courage. He hadn't thought they'd known about his meeting with the chief. If they'd found out about that, what else were they onto? Did they know he'd been trying to get in touch with outside help? Did they know about the A-Team?

'Three more months and they drop a pension in your lap, Maloney,' Stark continued. 'Don't be a chump. Take it and go find a nice place to settle down. You've earned it.'

'Yeah, Maloney,' Collins put in. 'Be a damn shame for you to go out in a tail spin, making a lot of false accusations and speculation about your fellow officers.'

Another sneeze overcame Maloney, and he almost fired his revolver trying to contain the force of the expulsion. Collins and Meadows ducked to one side, suspecting the sneeze was merely a diversion on Maloney's part. They whipped out their guns, but Maloney held back from firing at them. Trying to focus his attention solely on the group's spokesman, he told Stark, 'If you thought all I had was speculations, we wouldn't be sharing the night air out here right now, would we?'

Collins crunched gravel under the soles of his boots as he stepped past Stark and glared at Maloney. His brows arched and lowered over his eyes like small bears at the edge of a cliff. 'We're the police. We serve and protect,' he drawled coyly, letting his gaze fall on the sizeable bulge in Maloney's pocket. 'If something were to happen to us, why, who knows what might happen to all those nice, innocent people out there.'

As Collins peered past Maloney at the distant, winking lights of Simi, Stark finished the threat. 'People like your old lady, Ed ... and your daughter.'

'Leave them out of this,' Maloney insisted.

'Too late,' Stark said.

'What do you mean?' Maloney's voice quavered slightly and he felt suddenly weak in the knees. Not his family. They wouldn't dare. Renewed fears spawned a bead of sweat on his brow, and it rolled hotly down into his eye, stinging it. He braced himself against the pain, not wanting to take his eyes off the four men before him. He watched as Collins handed Stark a packet roughly the same size as the folder Maloney had secreted beneath the front seat of his Plymouth. Stark, in turn, tossed the packet at Maloney who caught it with his free hand.

'Be easier for you to look at them with both hands,' Stark advised him. 'Cut down on the chances we'll have to vent you, too. Give us all a break, okay?'

Maloney hesitated a moment, then let go of his gun and took his hand out of his pocket so he could open the packet. Inside were a series of snapshots depicting two women. One was Maloney's wife. The other was his daughter. The photos showed them going about their daily business, obviously unaware that their pictures were being taken. Maloney's daughter was captured on film in a college setting, while her mother was shown at a local supermarket and leaving her office job in Simi. As he flipped through the pictures, Maloney's heart sank. Some of the pictures were over a week old. If they'd been onto him for that long, it wasn't likely that he'd managed to engage in his search for the A-Team without them knowing about it.

'The crime rate's something awful around that university, they tell me,' Collins remarked, noting the changed expression on Maloney's face as he looked at the snapshots of his daughter. 'Wouldn't want something to happen to a cute-looking item like that. It'd be a shame, a real shame.'

Maloney looked up slowly from the photos, rage wrestling with the fear inside him. His throat was too tight for him to speak, so he could only gaze hatefully at the four men as they got back into the patrol car. Meadows started up the engine and killed the overhead light. After waiting for traffic to clear, he slowly eased the car forward. Riding shotgun, Stark rolled down his window as they passed Maloney and offered a final warning. 'Forget talking to the Captain tomorrow. And don't think we won't hear about it if you do. After all, we're all part of the same team.'

'Bastards,' Maloney sputtered, finding his voice. 'Harm my family and you'll pay, all of you!'

'Well, now, that's up to you, friend, isn't it?' Stark said, rolling up his window. 'Think about it.'

Meadows floored the accelerator and the patrol car screeched off into the night. Maloney stood and watched the retreating tail-lights until they were gone from view, then glanced back down at the packet of photos. He felt helpless, vulnerable, a failure to those who loved and depended on him. Where did he come off thinking he was being a hero? Who did he think he was kidding, anyway? An honest cop. Big deal. Be honest and your family's as good as dead, he thought to himself as he trudged wearily back to his car. Of course, who was to say that if he followed Stark's advice and kept his mouth shut that it would be any different for him. Maybe some day he'd pile his family into the car to go to a ballgame and a bomb would go off with the ignition. There didn't seem to be any way to get out of the situation he'd wandered into. Whatever he did, he felt sure he could only lose.

'What a life,' he murmured, sliding in behind the wheel of his Plymouth. For several long minutes he stayed there, unmoving, then he finally started up the car and drove off. He was ready for that drink now.

ONE

Hannigan's Bar was a low-profile drinking hole wedged between a donut shop and an all-night bail bonds office in a small shopping plaza located a few blocks from Ed Maloney's home. A black-and-white television set was propped up in a corner behind the bar, throwing off the luminous glow of old cop show reruns for the amusement of the bartender and the two tight-lipped men nursing mixed drinks at the counter. A few yards away, three younger men crowded around a battered dart board, trying for bullseyes between sips from their once-frosted mugs. When the jukebox behind them finished a song and went idle for lack of quarters, the dart players drained their beers and strolled to the exit, psyching themselves up for the envisioned lovelies they hoped would be waiting for them at a singles bar down the street. The last one out held the door open for Ed Maloney, who dabbed at his running nose with a handkerchief as he sulked his way to the nearest barstool.

'Gimme a draught, Mick,' he groaned to the bartender, who was dividing his time between cleaning mugs and watching Sgt Joe Friday wrap up tonight's episode of 'Dragnet' with the able, deadpan assistance of Officer Bill Gannon.

'Ed!' Mick called out, stacking the last of the mugs and then flinging his drenched towel over the nearest draught spigot. When he spied the burdensome expression on Maloney's face, the bartender stopped smiling and sauntered over, assuming his relished role as resident counsellor. Although he was, in fact, several years younger than Maloney, Mick took on a parental tone as he continued, in a thick brogue borrowed from his ancestors, 'My, and look at the sight of you! You're lookin' like the problems of all time are weighin' ya down, I'm like to tell you. And what's this with the leakin' sniffer, now? It sounds like you haven't been takin' such fine care of yourself, lad ...'

'Give it a rest, Mick,' Maloney countered gruffly, slapping a few dollars on the counter. 'I'm not in the mood for the Father Flannery schtick tonight, okay? Just get my beer and get ready to keep 'em coming.'

Maloney's foul mood swelled throughout the bar, and the other two men promptly left to make room for it. Mick let out a dreary sigh as he pulled a fresh mug out of the freezer and set it under the tap. Dropping the flourish from his accent, he said, 'Your wife called twice lookin' for you, Ed. Sounded urgent, she did.'

A flash of concern burned through Maloney, but he quickly surmised that if Stark and the others had been following him around most of the night, they couldn't have been keeping his family under surveillance. His wife was probably just concerned because he was late getting home. He'd mentioned running a few errands down in the city, but he'd said he'd be home by nine. It was now past ten-thirty.

'Need some change for the phone?' Mick asked him as he brought a foaming mug over to Maloney.

Shaking his head dully, Maloney took the beer and tilted it to his lips, giving himself a foam moustache as he downed the cold brew. Mick eyed him warily, then busied himself with cleaning off the counter as Maloney slid off his stool and ambled over to the pay phone on the wall. He called home, but the line was busy. He briefly considered having the operator cut in to make sure there was somebody on the phone, but finally decided that if his wife or daughter were interrupted in the middle of a call they would only be alarmed. He didn't want them to know what was going on. He hung up and decided to try calling again after he finished his beer.

On his way back to the bar, Maloney noticed the main door swing inward, admitting a middle-aged, swaggering figure who looked like someone who'd just failed to last three minutes in the ring with Bongo the Boxing Kangaroo.

'Ach, not you again ...' Mick grumbled at the man. 'Back like a bad habit, are you?'

The newcomer shuffled his way to the bar, pausing every few steps to pummel the air with a clumsy combination of lefts and rights. If a bug had been flying in the path of his fists, it might have been stunned, at best.

'Hiya, Mick!' the man chirped merrily, brushing a lock of greying hair from his eyes. He momentarily regarded Maloney, then resumed his haranguing of the bartender, thumping a calloused fist on the countertop. 'How s'bout s'more suds for ol' Kid Shaleen, eh?'

Maloney sneered at the weathered boxer and shifted on his stool to inch away from him. Mick ran Maloney's cash through the register and returned with a handful of change before circling around the bar, rolling up his sleeves to reveal a respectable bit of bicep. 'Now, come on, Kid,' he told the boxer with strained patience. 'I thought I sent ya t'home an hour ago. Get lost on the way, did you?'

'Home?' The boxer creased his face and made as if to spit on the floor with disgust. 'A coupla busted springs on legs at the Y? Ya call that a home? When I was the champ, suites at the Hilton was my style. Room service, hot 'n' cold runnin' booze 'n' broads ... ice in the terlets ...' Memories clouded the man's eyes and made his smile loopier by the moment. 'I was doin' it then, I'll be tellin' ya. Hey, Mick, did I tell ya how I put away that Valdez chap? Third round down in TJ?'

Mick nodded indulgently as the boxer backpedalled towards the service door near the back corner, bobbing his shoulders stiffly and assuming the vague semblance of a boxer's crouch. 'Yeah, yeah, Kid. You told me at least twice already tonight. How about once more, then be on your way, eh? That's a lad.'

Encouraged, the boxer winked and boasted, 'Well, since I told ya, I got no need for play-by-play commentary. Lemme just show ya the razzle-dazzle I used ta put 'im on ice ...'

As the man began recklessly stalking his unseen adversary, Maloney and Mick traded glances. Mick shrugged his shoulders, disavowing any keen insight into the pathetic exhibition they were being subjected to. Appearances were deceiving, though, and during that brief moment when the other men had their eyes off him, a glimmer of concentration came to the eyes of the boxer. He feigned a stumble, propelling himself against the service door long enough to reach out and slide the thick deadbolt out of place, opening the way to the side alley. Diversion accomplished, he staggered wildly back to the middle of the bar, grunting arduously from the supposed impact of his ineffectual punches on the ghost of Valdez.

'Did ya see that combo, there?' he beamed at his audience. 'Right, left, right, right. Kapow! Ha! Down he went, out cold. Third round! Don't get me wrong, though. That was one tough Mex ... even odds, that's how they were bettin' on us when we stepped inta the ring. Ah, Tijuana ...'

Maloney had seen enough. Pity overcame his annoyance and he left the counter to approach the boxer, telling him, 'Okay, okay, my friend. We get the picture. Don't wear yourself out, there.' Patting the other man on the back, Maloney called out to the bartender, 'Mick, get this guy a beer, on me. I'll have another, too.'

'Ah, a man after me own heart!' the boxer said as Maloney guided him over to one of the booths located near the hallway leading from the service entrance to the bar's stockroom. The boxer's gait went awry several times, and he clung to Maloney for additional support, at the same time keeping the officer's back to the door and hallway as he blathered loudly, 'I'm tellin' ya, when –'

'Before you tell me anything,' Maloney interrupted, 'how's about sitting down before anybody gets hurt, all right? We'll share a round, then I'll make a quick call and drop you off at the Y on my way home. How's that for a plan?'

'Hmmmmm ...' As he mulled over the proposition, the boxer glanced over his shoulder. The office phone had just rung, and Mick was ducking into the back room behind the bar to answer it, leaving the other two men alone. The boxer suddenly shed his punchdrunk demeanor and clamped his hands firmly around Maloney's arm.

'Hey, what the –'

'Okay, Inspector, let's go have ourselves a chat,' the boxer said with firm assurance, cutting off Maloney's protest and leading him down the back hall to the storage room.

'Who are you?' Maloney sputtered, trying to balance himself and shake the other man's grip on his arm.

'I'm Hannibal Smith,' the boxer told him. 'You said you wanted to hire the A-Team?'

'The A-Team!' Maloney gasped. 'Yeah, but what does –'

'Then let's step into my office and talk business.' Hannibal reached behind him with his free hand and opened the door to the stockroom. He let go of Maloney and gestured inside. Maloney paused a moment, still trying to make sense of the recent turn of events, then reluctantly went into the cramped enclosure. He wished he'd left his gun in his coat pocket instead of switching it back to his holster before driving to the bar. He didn't think he'd be able to get to it if the need arose. Hannibal followed Maloney inside and closed the door behind him, just as Mick was emerging from the office. The bartender puzzled over the sudden disappearance of his patrons, but the arrival of a few new customers kept him from investigating the matter further.

If Maloney was disconcerted by the manner of his introduction to Hannibal Smith, the looming presence of a second member of the A-Team in the storage room gave him an even more potent jolt of adrenalin. BA Baracus, black-hewed and dressed in a cutoff jumpsuit and a near-blinding array of gold jewellery, stared at the officer with a scowl made more menacing by the off-centre Mohawk lining the top of his shaved head. As BA took a step forward and quickly frisked Maloney, relieving him of his gun, Hannibal handled the introductions.

'BA, this is Ed Maloney, the gentleman we were supposed to meet down in San Pedro. Ed, meet BA Baracus. BA stands for Bad Attitude, so don't think he's singling you out with that cheery mug of his. He looks at everyone like that.'

'Uh, hi.' Maloney gathered his wits and offered to shake

BA's hand. Anything to buy time. He had no idea what was going on around him. Baracus only stared at the man's hand, though, before tossing the revolver to Hannibal and then crossing his arms like a Nubian guard standing watch before the entrance to a king's ransom.

As he calmly shook open the chamber on Maloney's revolver and tapped out the bullets, Hannibal said, 'Sorry about things being so hectic, Inspector, but I'm sure you understand.'

Maloney didn't understand. He sneezed, then reached for his handkerchief. Hannibal reached out and grabbed him, then checked Maloney's pocket to make sure he wasn't hiding a second gun before letting go. Maloney blew his nose, then complained, 'I all but gave up on you guys. I waited at the pier down in San Pedro like that Mister Lee said. Three hours I waited, and all I got was this cold. I figured you guys weren't up for the job.'

'We aren't up for working for no police,' BA growled.

With more tact, Hannibal explained, 'Mr Maloney, when you showed up at the pier, you had some of your boyfriends in tow. They were trying to be discreet, but we didn't have much trouble spotting them. Now, we weren't about to show ourselves and risk finding ourselves caught up in —'

'I came down there alone, damn it!' Maloney insisted. 'Look, I was put onto you guys by a reliable source and ... hold on, wait a minute. These guys you thought were backing me up ... were there four of them? In a cruiser?'

'Gee, I don't know, Inspector, why don't you tell us?' Hannibal said.

'Those are the guys I want you to help me finger!' Maloney exclaimed, raising his voice from a whisper to compete with the thumping bass line sounding from the activated jukebox on the other side of the wall. 'They must have followed me all the way down there and back. I just had a confrontation with them on the way here. They're trying to put the fear on me by threatening my wife and kid. If they weren't afraid that I have some evidence hiding somewhere, they probably would have given me a lead shower and dumped me in the aqueduct for a quick trip back to the harbour.'

As Hannibal and BA weighed Maloney's story, there was a light rapping of knuckles on the stockroom door, followed immediately by the arrival of Templeton Peck, who looked like a male model who'd just finished a day of shooting men's fashions for Gentleman's Quarterly. He nodded greetings to Hannibal and BA, then told Maloney, with a winsome grin, 'They call me Face. Don't ask me why.'

'And you three make up the A-Team?' Maloney said.

'Well, we have two other members who help out when they can,' Hannibal said, 'but we're the nucleus. We're the ones that decide if a certain job's worth taking ... or whether it might be a trap, say, with the military police ...'

'I'm a city cop,' Maloney said, easing back against a stack of beer cases to make room for Face. 'I haven't dealt with the military since Korea. As for a trap, if I were thinking of ways to lure you behind bars, I think I could come up with a better story than the one I came to Mr Lee with. Let's face it, who'd be apt to believe there's men off a SWAT team that do hits for hire on the side?'

'Good question,' Hannibal admitted. 'It *is* a crazy story, all right ... just crazy enough to be true. Which I guess is why we're here to get a few more details.'

'What do you want to know?'

'Why do you want us?' Hannibal asked. 'Seems to me that cops like to clean their own house when it starts to stink. Why aren't you having this handled through Internal Affairs?'

Maloney looked the other three men over, wondering if he wanted to divulge any more information than he already had. When he'd been told initially about the A-Team by a close friend who'd heard of their exploits, he'd pictured a different sort of crew, something along the lines of khaki-clad commandoes. His rendezvous with Mr Lee, the bumbling proprietor of a Chinese laundromat near the police station, had given him his first misgivings about the people he proposed to deal with. Now, seeing the team in the flesh, he wondered how much of their reputation was hyperbole and how much had any foundation in reality. These three men seemed more suited to street theatre than

19

the kind of venture he was proposing.

'We're waiting, Inspector,' Hannibal said, pulling a wrapped cigar from his pocket and slowly peeling away the cellophane. 'Let's have it. What makes these hit men click, and why don't you sic IA on them if they're as much of a danger as you claim they are?'

'I can't go to Internal Affairs because that's where it all began,' Maloney finally divulged. 'Stark, the brains behind it all, worked his way up to Captain out of IA, and in the process he managed to get some choice goods on the three others. The kind of dirt that could have cost them their badges. When he switched over to SWAT, he got them transferred to his command. They put up quite a front. As SWAT officers, they've got one of the hottest records on the force. Especially when it comes to marksmanship.'

'A nice cover,' Hannibal reflected.

'I still don't like it,' BA said. 'If we gotta be on the run from the law, we gotta be stupid to start doing them any favours.'

'Now, now, BA,' Face interjected. 'Don't forget all the good deeds we've been doing to polish our image. This sounds like something that would look real nice on our resume.'

'Quit jokin', man,' BA warned Face.

'Knock it off, both of you,' Hannibal told his cohorts. When Face and BA fell silent beneath the dull glow of the bulb dangling from the ceiling, he turned back to Maloney and said, 'So far, so good. Now tell me exactly what these guys have done. By hit men, I assume you mean –'

'– they've killed at least seven people that I know of,' Maloney affirmed. 'It wouldn't surprise me if they've handled more contracts, and it wouldn't surprise me if there are more officers implicated down the line. That's why I've come to you. I need help. Something has to be done.' Going slowly through his coat pockets so that they wouldn't think he was reaching for a weapon, Maloney pulled out two small manilla packets. He gave the one with the snapshots to Face, saying, 'They warned me tonight that they'd hurt my wife and daughter if I went to Chief Metcalf. I'm supposed to see him tomorrow, but all I have are allegations. No proof. I

20

doubt that he'll believe me.'

'A safe bet,' Face agreed as he scanned the photos and then handed them to Hannibal. 'I don't think anyone would.'

'I sure don't,' BA said. 'It's gotta be some kinda trap, Hannibal. This guy's a cop!'

'Hey, look!' Maloney snapped back angrily, 'If you don't want the job then what are you doing here? I've spent time roaming alleys, dealing with that Confucian dingbat Mr Lee, catching cold at the docks in San Pedro ... just so that you can stand back and call me a liar?'

'Inspector ...' Hannibal said. 'Keep it down. I haven't paid any rent on this office suite, and I'd hate to get evicted before we've settled this ...'

'The hell with it,' Maloney snarled, tearing open the second envelope, revealing a thick stack of fifty dollar bills. 'Here, my life savings, backing up my word.' He handed the money to Face, who began to count it, then resumed, 'I'll tell you right now, up front. I *am* a cop. A good one, too. If I wasn't up against a wall, I wouldn't be dealing with outlaws like you. My buddy put me onto you, said you were my best shot. Now I'm beginning to wonder.'

Peck finished counting the bills, then told Hannibal, 'Fourteen thousand, six hundred and two dollars ...'

'That's all I got,' Maloney said. 'I can show you my bank books if you don't believe me.'

'That's not necessary,' Hannibal told him, taking the money from Face and eyeing it.

'I know Mister Lee said you charged more,' Maloney said. 'A lot more. But what you've got there represents every cent Edward Maloney's managed to save in his life. If you want the job you take that. If you don't want it, give me the money back, good-bye and good luck and I'll take my best shot with the Chief in the morning.'

The air was getting hot in the congested room. Maloney's tough facade was ruptured by still another sneeze while BA, Face and Hannibal conferred with glances a few moments. When they'd reached an unspoken decision, Hannibal looked back to Maloney and said, 'With no proof, it'll be your word against four other police officers.'

'And what about your family?' Face put in.

'I'll do what I have to take care of them,' Maloney said with determination. 'I've been a cop too damn long to let those scumbags drag my kind through the dirt. Like I said, if you can't help me, or won't, then let me outta here so I can start doing what I can on my own.'

'What would you expect us to do, Inspector?' Hannibal asked, as patient as ever. 'Assuming we take your payment and give it a crack, what kind of help can you give us for starters? I don't think we're going to be able to find a little black book that'll put the finger on them, do you?'

Maloney's spirits rose slightly at the prospect of help. 'No, but if one of them could be convinced to confess, that might do it. You know, get one of them to turn state's evidence for a lighter sentence. We have to try something!'

Hannibal put the money in his pocket and the unwrapped cigar in his mouth, then snatched up the .38 revolver and bullets from the beer keg he'd set them on and handed them back to Maloney. 'We'll see what we can do. Why don't you hold off seeing Metcalf and just go about your business like you've let them scare you off. Maybe we can give them enough rope to hang themselves.'

'I'd like to help out some way,' Maloney said, slipping the unloaded gun into his holster and the bullets into his coat pocket. 'At least keep me posted on what you're doing, won't you?'

'Let me make something clear, Inspector,' Hannibal told him. 'We play by our own rules or we don't play at all. Just give us some room, okay? We'll be in touch if we think it's necessary. For now, why don't you go tell Mick you took Kid Shaleen out to catch a cab, then have yourself another drink before you head home. Your nerves are a mess.'

'Yeah, yeah, I guess you're right.' Maloney backed away from the members of the A-Team and reached for the door behind him. 'Thanks, guys. Sorry I gave you such a hard time. Like you said, nerves. Thanks again.'

'Thank us when it's over,' Hannibal suggested. 'Until then, we've got a lot of work cut out for us ...'

TWO

While Maloney was distracting Mick at the bar, the three members of the A-Team slipped out the side entrance and made their way down the alley to the back parking lot, where BA's black van gleamed under the glow of security lights. A wind had picked up over the past hour, rustling leaves in the surrounding lots and sending stray bits of litter dancing across the darkened asphalt.

'That Maloney's one tough dude, ain't he?' BA conceded as he fumbled through his jumpsuit pockets for keys and unlocked the doors to the van.

'Irish grit,' Hannibal said, climbing into the cushioned interior of what constituted the A-Team's rolling headquarters, base of operations, and occasional crash pad, depending on circumstances.

'I tell ya, Hannibal,' Face commented, 'those photos they took of his wife and daughter would have put the best paparazzi to shame. If they'd have been shooting bullets instead of pictures, it would have been all over for the Maloney family. I can't believe they got those close up shots off without being seen. These guys aren't slouches.'

'Neither are we,' Hannibal said confidently, finally setting a match to the tip of his cigar and filling the van with aromatic fumes. He braced himself as BA backed out of their parking space and drove down the alley, then sped out onto the street. Taking the cigar out and waving it with a flourish, he remarked, 'We're off the bricks again, gents.'

BA shook his head and curled his lips into a sneer as he navigated the next corner and headed back for the freeway. 'Workin' for the police. Man, I can't believe it!'

'Hey, BA,' Hannibal reassured him, 'Just because we have a small problem with one arm of the law is no reason to cop an attitude.'

'"*Cop* an attitude",' BA spat. 'You tryin' to be funny, Hannibal? I ain't in the mood for no dumb puns, man.'

'All I'm saying is that all cops aren't like Lynch.'

'Ah, Lynch. Dear, sweet Lynch,' Face reflected, conjuring up the image of their arch nemesis, an Army Colonel who'd spent most of the past ten years trying to track down the A-Team after they escaped from confinement at Fort Bragg. What a ten years it had been for the A-Team. Living on the lam, usually hiding out in the LA underground, they'd dispelled their boredom by taking on a wide range of death-defying assignments for an equally diverse range of hard-luck individuals, earning for themselves in the process a reputation that was part Robin Hood and his Merry Men, part Nick Fury and his Howling Commandoes, and part Dirty Dozen. They were mercenaries, soldiers for hire, rebels with a cause ... clearing their names and hopefully their records of the false charges that had led to their imprisonment back in Fort Bragg.

'Workin' for the cops,' BA muttered again.

'When I was a kid, I always wanted to be a policeman,' Face blurted out, earning incredulous glances from his counterparts. 'I'm serious,' he went on. 'In the orphanage, I had a whole scrapbook of Dick Tracy and his crime stopper's text. My favourite show was "Dragnet". Heck, I learned most of my cons from the episodes about bunco artists.'

'How touching,' Hannibal drawled. 'Too bad you weren't by Hannigan's earlier. I think one of those shows was on. Which reminds me, did anything interesting happen while you were casing out Maloney's place?'

Face shook his head. 'My leg fell asleep from the way I was sitting up in that tree. There was a cop car that rolled by an hour ago, but it didn't stop near the house. The daughter

24

came home from school a little after that and no one was tailing her.'

'That makes sense, especially if Maloney was on the level about the four of them being the ones BA and I spotted down at San Pedro.' Hannibal pried open the dashboard ashtray and deposited a load from the tip of his cigar as he stared out at the road ahead of them. They were coming up on the freeway now, gaining speed by the second.

'So how do we shut these guys down, Hannibal?' BA asked as he veered the van around a chuckhole the size of a trashcan lid. Face hadn't been watching, and he almost fell off his seat with the force of the swerve. BA continued, 'These turkeys are SWAT, man, trained in special weapons and tactics.'

'I think we know what it stands for, BA,' Face said glibly.

'Yeah, well, that's our gig,' BA countered. 'It's gonna be like going up against ourselves.'

'Isometrics, BA. Isometrics,' Hannibal said. 'Best kind of exercise there is. One muscle against the other.'

'Yeah, but when you do isometrics, both muscles end up gettin' stronger, man,' BA complained. 'We gotta come up with a way that puts us on top. We gotta have an edge.'

'I'm sure we'll think of something,' Hannibal ventured.

'We better start thinkin' fast,' BA said, reaching the speed limit and then flipping the cruise control into service. 'Maybe we oughta start trailing them the same way they've been following that cop's wife and daughter.'

'Hmmmmmmm.' Hannibal eased back in his seat and blew a few smoke rings, eyeing them with the concentration of a mystic probing the depths of a crystal ball. A smile slowly came to his lips. 'I think you're on the right track, BA. But, like you say, we've got to go one better to get an edge.'

'Something tells me you've already got something in mind,' Face said, clamping on his seat belt against the chance BA might start swerving again.

'BA, are you still tinkering around with miniaturised electronics?' Hannibal asked.

'Yeah.'

Hannibal smiled again. 'Then I have a plan ...'

THREE

It was days like that that made Amy Allen begin to wonder why she'd managed to talk herself into being a part-time member of the A-Team. It wasn't like she didn't have enough work to keep her busy without them. Her job at the Los Angeles Courier-Express was a demanding one, often requiring fourteen-hour workdays in the pursuit of a story she could feel proud about putting her byline on. Reporting gave her plenty of opportunities to have her fill of excitement, intrigue, danger, and all the things restless souls crave for. So why did she find herself seeking more?

'Must be for the jazz,' she grumbled half-heartedly, stifling a yawn as she weaved her way through morning traffic choking the heart of LA. She'd come home from work at three in the morning to find a small package in her mail-box, along with a note from BA briefly describing the A-Team's newest venture and asking her to lend them a hand this morning in the first phase of their mission. She wasn't sure what the plan was, but she felt confident it would prove to be as off-the-wall as most of the others she'd participated in the past few months. Nursing a mug of steaming coffee, she followed the flow of commuters until she reached her designated turnoff and left the freeway for the less-congested traffic of side streets. She'd travelled these roads only a few days ago while working on a story for the paper, so she had no trouble finding the small park where she was supposed to rendezvous with Templeton Peck.

It was a little before seven-thirty. Amy had made better time than she thought, and she had a few minutes before Face was due to come by to pick her up. She finished her coffee and fidgeted with the radio dial, trying to find something more listenable than the manic prattle of loudmouthed disc jockeys. Tuning into a classical station, she relaxed to the soothing strains of a Beethoven sonata and closed her eyes against the glare of the just-risen sun. Fatigue caught up with her and was luring her to sleep when a strange-sounding horn bleated loudly next to her, jolting her abruptly back to consciousness.

A white panel truck rolled past Amy and eased to a halt alongside the kerb in front of her car. Stencilled lettering on the truck's siding read 'DROP DEAD PEST CONTROL', and propped on the roof was a goliath plastic insect that looked like a cross between a termite and a six-limbed Sumo wrestler. The driver opened his door at the same time as Amy and leaned out to grin back at her. It was Templeton Peck, wearing uniform-like coveralls and grinning as he held out another pair to Amy.

'Mornin', love bug,' he greeted her. 'How's about slipping into something comfortable?'

Amy ignored Face's conspiratorial wink and wearily snatched the second pair of coveralls from him. Yawning again, she climbed into the outfit. It barely fit. 'This is wonderful. I always wanted to be an exterminator.'

'Temper temper, Amy,' Face scolded lightly. 'Think of the symbolic irony.'

'It's a little early in the day for symbolic irony, Face.' Amy circled around the front of the truck and climbed up into the passenger seat. As Face shifted gears and pulled out into the street, Amy looked behind her seat to inspect the truck's interior, remarking, 'Say, didn't we use this as a bread truck a couple months ago when we were rescuing that British diplomat from the IRA terrorists?'

Face nodded proudly as he turned the next corner. 'Yep. And before that we dolled it up to run a sting on some con-artists peddling fake French antiques. It's amazing what a coat of paint and a little ingenuity can do, isn't it?'

'Speaking of ingenuity, why couldn't you guys handle things this morning without me? I'm beat. Where's Hannibal and BA anyway?'

'They've got their own work cut out for them,' Face explained. 'We couldn't get Murdock on this short of notice, so that left you. Besides, we might need a little charm to pull this off, and you're tops in that department.'

'That's it, when all else fails, lay on the flattery.' Amy shifted in her seat, adjusting the coverall suspenders to make herself more comfortable.

'Well, here we are.' Peck turned one last corner and brought the truck to a stop in front of the large, nondescript building that housed the Police Department's SWAT unit and its arsenal of weaponry. A couple officers were out in front, running a flag up the pole and watching it unfurl in the morning breeze.

'Okay, I'm ready,' Amy said. They got out of the truck and went around to the back. As Face was throwing open the doors, Amy told him, 'If we pull this off without a hitch, I get the rest of the day off to nap, right?'

'Deal.' Face rummaged through the back of the truck, coming up with a pair of cannisters containing compressed carbon dioxide. Taking a roll of labels from a small shipping box by the wheel well, he peeled off two stickers and slapped them onto the cannisters, declaring them to be pesticide dispensers. 'I "borrowed" these from the same place I got the bug on the roof. Now, do you have that kit BA dropped off last night?'

Amy reached into her blouse pocket and withdrew a flat, rectangular case, showing it to Peck before transferring it to her coveralls. 'I still can't believe this is going to work, though.'

'Sure it's gonna work,' Face insisted. 'Everybody hates roaches. Speaking of which . . .' Before closing the rear doors of the truck, Peck pulled out a small jar and handed it to Amy. The jar was filled with cockroaches of various sizes, all of them scurrying madly about as if trying to find shelter from the sunlight. 'Here, Amy, put this in your pocket.'

'In my pocket?!' Amy gasped, cringing from the sight of

the roaches. 'Look, this is where I draw the line . . .'

'Quick, before anybody sees. Let's get serious here.'

'I've got to be out of my mind,' Amy said, testing to make sure the lid was screwed on tight before slipping the jar into another pocket in her coveralls. 'Yech!'

Entering the SWAT headquarters, Peck and Amy slipped quickly into character and made their way halfway down the main corridor before being intercepted by a lean, be-spectacled sergeant with thick blond hair and piercing brown eyes. He demanded, 'And just where the hell do you two think you're going?'

Face spotted the entrance to the officers' locker room and veered towards it as he told the sergeant, 'I'm from Drop Dead. We got a call to come and take care of your cockroach infestation.' Referring to notes he'd scribbled on clipboard earlier, he went on, 'They said it's worst in the locker rooms, so we'll start there.'

'Cockroaches?' the sergeant said, lengthening his stride to keep up with Face and Amy. 'We don't have any cockroaches here, for cryin' out loud. What is this, some kinda joke?'

'Vermin are no joking matter, sergeant,' Amy said somberly as Peck pushed through the entrance to the locker room. The officer followed him in and held the door open for Amy.

Peck suddenly pivoted about to face the sergeant, putting on a show of impatience. 'Look, pal, your custodian put me through all kinds of hell setting up this inspection, telling me I had to be down here this morning before things got any more out of hand than they already have.'

'Well, I doubt that anything's out of hand, because I haven't seen one of those suckers around there, and I've been here seven years,' the sergeant declared. 'It must have been Louie that called you, but he doesn't come in for an hour and I don't have anything from anybody saying you were coming. You can't be in here without proper authorization.'

Peck let out a huff and planted his hands on his hips, becoming increasingly annoyed with the situation. Looking over the sergeant's shoulder, he had to struggle to keep up the facade as he saw Amy busily trying to liberate the cockroaches from the jar without them crawling onto her hand. Seeing that she needed more time, Face raised his voice to hold the sergeant's attention. 'Hey, my work day usually doesn't start for another hour. You think I get my rocks off bug-hunting at this hour? Your man Louie said I had to be in and outta here before the day shift came on, so here I am, ready, willing and able, and you tell me I gotta leave because Louie didn't leave you a note. Well, fine, pal. Fine. We get paid for a service call regardless.'

'Now just a second ...' the sergeant protested.

With considerable difficulty, Amy finally was able to convince one of the cockroaches to start roaming the shoulder of the officer. The insect trekked down to the man's chevrons, then changed course and headed for his breast pocket. Noticing the roach's manoeuvre, Face took quick action, holding out his clipboard and saying, 'If I could just get your signature here, sergeant? I don't want Louie to think I didn't show up. Sorry, but I don't have a pen on me ...'

Reaching to his shirt pocket for a pen, the sergeant said, 'I'll sign, but don't think we're going to pay if this turns out to be nothing but a false alllllllaaaaieeee!' He cut his sentence short with a shriek as the errant cockroach scrambled from his uniform to his fingers and began wading through the hairs on the back of his hand like a grain farmer treading through a field of wheat. The officer shook his hand desperately until the insect was jarred loose and fell to the floor, where its comrades were already bounding across the linoleum for cover.

'What the hell?!!' the sergeant exclaimed with disbelief.

Face whistled lowly and shook his head. 'Those look like breeding reds. Probably come out of the baseboards.'

'Look at them!' The officer lashed out with his size twelve Florsheims and flattened one of the bugs. 'I've never seen 'em before this!'

'It's a bad sign when they start running around in the open like this,' Face told him. 'Means they have no more crawl space in the walls. Probably laid all their eggs and need more room. That's when they usually wind up going for any place else around that's dark and cool.'

'Like the lockers,' Amy suggested as she discreetly sidestepped the crushed cockroach near the officer's foot.

'The lockers?'

'That's right,' Face affirmed. 'You might want to tell the guys to shake out their uniforms before they suit up. Have them check inside their caps, too. Those little bastards can be murder if they get in your hair.'

'Oh, man ...' The sergeant's hand went reflexively to his head. He ran his fingers through his hair, checking his scalp, looking suddenly worried.

Amy put her hand to her mouth to keep from laughing. When she brought herself under control, she observed, 'I don't want to be an alarmist, officer, but there's a chance you could already be bringing them home with you. Be careful, these are germ carriers.'

'What kind of germs?' The authority was gone from the sergeant's voice. Ensnarled by a growing phobia, he swallowed hard, rubbing the back of his hand on his pants in hopes of wiping off any trace of disease the cockroach might have left during its brief jaunt on his flesh.

Face winked at Amy, then told the sergeant, 'You also probably should ask the guys if any of them have experienced any symptoms ... like a harsh taste in their mouths?'

'A h ... harsh taste?' The officer licked his lips and Face could see the man working his tongue around the inside of his mouth. 'You know, in the morning, sometimes –'

'In the morning, you bet,' Face said before turning to Amy. 'Well, partner, since we're outta here, we might as well slide over to Gower and handle that other call ...'

'The Hip Bagel?' Amy said. 'I don't think there'll be anyone there yet.'

'Hey, hey,' the sergeant said. 'Listen, since Louie already set up an appointment and you're already here, why don't you just go ahead and do your spraying or whatever. But I got roll call in twenty minutes, so I need you out of here in fifteen.'

Face and Amy looked at one another, as if debating

31

whether or not to take on the job. They finally nodded in unison and Face patted his cannister confidently as he assured the officer, 'No problem. This here's great new stuff. Had a chemist working on it for the past fourteen years. Only the bugs'll smell it.'

'Great!' The sergeant headed for the door, then stopped and looked back at Face and Amy. 'Uh ... listen, if I gave you my address, I was wondering ... maybe you could stop by –'

'We'll get it on the way out,' Amy said.

Face piped in, 'Better dead than in your bed, eh, sarge?'

'Yeah, right.'

Once the officer was out the door, Face let out a breath of relief and Amy slumped against the row of lockers, shaking her head.

'I can't believe he fell for that,' she said.

'Hey, I told you it'd be a piece of cake,' Face countered. 'Now let's get cracking. Get that kit out and get ready to do your thing.'

There were names posted on each of the lockers, and Face went along the row until he found those belonging to the SWAT members they were trying to collar. Sitting on the bench before Stark's locker, he reached into his coveralls and came up with a lock pick and went to work tickling the tumblers. Amy sat down next to him and opened the case, which contained what appeared to be a sewing kit. By the time she had threaded one of the needles with a length of blue thread, Peck had sprung the first lock and opened the locker. Taking out one of Stark's uniform shirts, he handed it to Amy, saying, 'Okay, now replace one of the buttons with one in the kit. If you can do it with the collar, that'd be best.'

As she carefully pried loose the button affixed to the uniform collar, Amy snorted with mock contempt, 'Bringing me along to do the sewing is very sexist, you know.'

'We each do what we have to,' Face responded, sliding down the bench to tackle the next locker. 'Now, if you think you can pick these three locks in three minutes ...'

'All right, all right,' Amy said. 'If I knew this was all I was going to do, though, I would have stayed in bed and sent my grandmother ...'

32

FOUR

Tall palm trees threw long shadows across the parking lot as the day shift SWAT officers pulled into spaces shaded by the main building. Not surprisingly, most of the men drove muscle cars – new Mustangs, Datsun 280 Zs, souped-up Camaros and Firebirds – the kinds of cars their counterparts on the regular force wished they were able to drive on patrol instead of the wimp Matadors some clown had bought a fleet of a few years before. Dolph Stark screeched his custom Corvette into the lot, laughing loudly as he almost ran over Al Collins, who'd just gotten out of his Datsun.

'Mornin', Collins,' Stark called out. 'How they hangin'?'

'High and dry, my man,' Collins boomed back jovially, waiting for Stark to catch up with him. Once they were walking alongside one another towards the main entrance, they both lowered their voices and spoke in subdued whispers.

'So, I wonder if our friend Maloney's gonna try to be a hero today,' Collins speculated.

Stark shook his head. 'Don't think so. Shaeffer made a point of running into him when he left his house this morning. We scared that mick plenty. I think he'll clam up until we get around to silencing him for good.'

'I hope so.'

'Hey, relax, Collins. Get a little ice water pumping through those veins. We got a big day ahead of us.'

'Right. Today and tomorrow both.'

33

On their way to the front walkway, the two men passed the unattended Drop Dead Pest Control truck. Stark looked up at the company mascot and sniggered, 'Hey, check out that termite, will ya?'

'Hell, that isn't a termite. It's a cockroach.'

'No, no, wait ...' Stark took a step closer to the truck, scrutinizing the vehicle closely. He finally looked over his shoulder at Collins and said, 'Nope, I know what it is. It's like one of those crabs that's been feasting on your crotch the past few weeks.'

'Har har,' Collins replied, his voice thick with sarcasm.

A couple other officers fell in with Stark and Collins as they made their way inside the headquarters. The vending machines were at the opposite end of the corridor from the locker room, and the other two men parted ways with Stark and Collins in favour of tracking down cups of coffee. Once they were alone and heading down the hall towards the locker room, Collins snapped his fingers and whispered, 'Hey, I just came up with a great way to snuff somebody and make it look like an accident. Fumigate 'em!'

'Say what?'

'You heard me. Remember that guy over in Devonshire Division they found in a house that was covered up for termite spraying? They guessed he must have snuck in, thinking he could pull off an easy burglary, only he got himself gassed instead. Now, what we could do is nab whoever we've got a contract on, gag 'em and take 'em to –'

'Forget it, Collins,' Stark interrupted, shaking his head. 'Hell, that's too damn complicated. Too many ways to screw up. I say a quick bullet to the brain pan is still the best way to go. No muss, no fuss. Hit and run. Why knock success, eh?'

'Well,' Collins said after mulling it over, 'Maybe you're right ...'

'Of course I'm right,' Stark boasted, leaning into the door that led to the locker rooms. Carried by his own momentum, he lurched headlong into a cloud of pressurized carbon dioxide being sprayed by a cannister in the hands of Templeton Peck, who was wearing a surgical mask that made him look like Dr Ben Casey gone berserk. Collins wandered into the line of fire, too, and both men began instantly gasping for good air as their eyes teared and they clawed at the noxious cloud, trying to ward it away from their faces.

'Ah, gee, I'm sorry ... really I am,' Peck apologized, fumbling clumsily with the nozzle of the cannister as he tried to stem its gaseous flow. While maintaining this diversion, he shot a quick glance back at the row of lockers, where Amy was hastily stuffing a uniformed shirt into one of the cubicles and closing the door. Seeing that she still had to clamp the lock into place, Face unleashed another blast from the extinguisher and tried to herd Stark and Collins out of the room, telling them, 'I'm sorry, but this darn thing's gone on the fritz. You better clear out until this stuff thins out ...'

'We'll be okay once you quit spraying that crap in our faces,' Stark said between coughs, reaching out and pushing Peck's arms down so that he was gassing the floor instead. The cannister let out a final jet of carbon dixoide, then sputtered out. Both Stark and Collins went to their pants pockets, withdrawing handkerchiefs they used to wipe their faces.

'Hey, I don't know what to say,' Peck told them with supposed shame, still keeping his features half-hidden behind the surgical mask. Behind him, Amy clicked the lock shut and pulled her own mask up over her face.

'Don't say anything,' Stark said. 'Just get out before we give you a taste of your own medicine, damn you!'

'Yeah!' Collins added with equal annoyance. 'Why don't you watch what the hell you're doing with that thing? You're supposed to use it to spray bugs, aren't you?'

'That's right,' Face said, smiling behind the cover of his mask. 'Roaches and the like.'

Amy came up behind Face and told him, 'Well, I finished my end. I don't think they'll have too many more problems for awhile now.'

'We never had problems in the first place,' Collins told them.

Face pointed to the squashed cockroach on the floor. 'Well, that's certainly not an optical illusion.'

As Collins and Stark went over to inspect the tiny corpse, Face and Amy slipped out of the locker room and headed for the side exit.

'Whew, was that close!' Amy said.

'No kidding!' Peck reached the door first and held it open for Amy, continuing, 'I just hope those other cockroaches you let loose stay hidden for at least a few days. The less suspicions we raise, the better off we'll be.'

'Amen to that,' Amy said as they circled around the building and climbed into the exterminator truck. Peck started up the engine and pulled away, just as Adam Meadows turned into the parking lot, driving a Mazda RX-7 the colour of Paul Newman's eyes.

'Now all we have to do is track down Hannibal and BA,' Peck said, dividing his attention between the road before him and the cars parked along the kerb. After driving a few blocks, he smiled and slowed down, pointing at BA's black van, kerbed under the shade of a towering eucalyptus. 'There they are ...'

'This is awful close to the station, don't you think?' Amy remarked as Peck found a parking place on the other side of the street.

'Well, they wanted to get as close as they could until they got everything fine-tuned,' Peck explained as they both crossed the street and headed for the van. 'After they hone in on the signal, we can pull back quite a ways and still keep tabs on things.'

Hannibal had apparently seen them coming, and as they rounded the van, he threw open the side door to let them in. Puffing contentedly on a cigar, he was in high spirits, telling them, 'Nice job, kids. We're reading them loud and clear.'

'Gee, thanks, dad,' Peck shot back playfully as he and Amy nestled into the padded embrace of large cushions lying about the inside of the van. BA was seated on a bench next to a cluster of electronic equipment, including a monitor speaker and reel-to-reel tape recorder. He nodded a greeting to his fellow cohorts and raised a finger to his lips.

'Get an earful of this,' he whispered to them. Peck and Amy listened to the pair of voices coming in over the small

36

speakers.

'Hey, did you catch that game on the tube last night?'

'Sure as hell did. Last quarter, at any rate. Did the Lakers sock it to 'em or what?'

Peck muttered aloud, 'Yep, that's Stark and Collins, all right.' Turning to Amy he held out the flat of his palm and she lightly slapped it with her own. 'Good job, partner.'

'Doesn't that mean I get to take my nap?' Amy yawned.

BA took a pair of headphones out of a carrying case next to the recorder and plugged the jack into place, cutting off the voices coming in over the monitor. Putting the headphones on, he adjusted the volume so that he could hear both the conversation in the locker room and the one going on around him.

'BA's mini-mikes are coming in better than most radio stations I listen to,' Hannibal commented.

'I think I deserve a little credit for my sewing prowess,' Amy snickered.

'Right you are,' Face told her. 'You rate right up there, next to Betsy Ross.'

BA twirled a few more knobs on his control consoles, then estimated, 'Long as we stay within a one mile radius I figure the reception'll be good.'

'Have you picked up anything we can use yet?' Peck asked. 'Or are they just shooting the breeze?'

'Well, you can pick a lot out of the breeze if you listen right,' Hannibal observed. 'Now we know Stark, Collins, and Meadows are into any and all kinds of sports, and Collins is into anything that wears a skirt. A case of perpetual hots from the sounds of it. Also, Stark shacks up occasionally with some chick named Brenda Webb. I wonder if she's any relation to Jack?'

'I'll see if I can get an address and phone number back at the paper,' Amy volunteered. 'I'll even do it *before* I go home for my nap.'

'A true trooper,' Peck said.

'I think by the time we're done, we're going to need all the backup we can muster,' Hannibal said, looking at Peck. 'While you're out, how's about swinging by the VA Hospital and wrangling a furlough for Murdock?'

'Got it,' Peck said, opening the van door and hopping out.

'Hold it!' BA suddenly shouted, yanking off his headphones. 'Murdock? Why do we need that crazy fool? Man, we're not flying!'

'No one said anything about flying,' Peck told him.

'That's good, 'cause I ain't goin' near anything with wings, with or without Murdock,' BA declared. 'Murdock . . . man, that guy's certified fruit cake!'

'That's no way to talk about a guy who saved your butt at least a half-dozen times in Nam,' Hannibal reminded BA.

'Yeah, well . . .' BA grimaced at the thought of being indebted to the likes of Howling Mad Murdock. 'Maybe he saved my butt, that doesn't mean he's any less crazy . . .'

FIVE

'No one said anything about tuberculosis!'

The nurse accompanying Templeton Peck down the hallway of the patient ward at the Veteran's Administration Hospital was in the process of becoming unravelled. The possibility of one of her patients being afflicted with t.b. without her knowledge was a terrifying prospect. She pictured herself facing a medicinal tribunal in some dimlit chamber, destined to lose her job to charges of negligence and incompetence. In a last-ditch effort at self defence, she appealed to Face a final time.

'There was nothing on his chart. Surely we'd have noticed!'

Peck was wearing head-to-toe whites that contrasted sharply with his dark tan. He had the same surgical mask and clipboard he'd used during his brief performance as a pest exterminator at the SWAT station, but now he was assuming a different role. The nametag on his lapel declared him to be Dr Tenzig Hilli, Supervising Surgeon from the VA's regional headquarters. Whereas he had played the part of exterminator with an air of buffoonery, as Dr Hilli he was strictly no-nonsense, a man reeking of self-importance, a would-be hub around which the rest of the world was expected to revolve. A typical high-level bureaucrat.

'It showed up on his bi-annual,' Peck told the nurse, giving her a brief glance at the illegible scrawl adorning the medical form on his clipboard. Picking up his pace, he injected gravity into his voice, making himself out to be the last hope of salvation in the face of certain doom. 'With something as infectious and contagious as this we run the risk of a full-out epidemic. I just hope I'm here in time.'

'I don't know what to say,' the nurse murmured fraily, on the verge of tears. 'I tend to Mr Murdock nearly every day, and there've been no symptoms. I mean, I would have –'

'It's the Inherbi strain, nurse,' Peck lectured as he raised his surgical mask into position over his lower features. 'A rare virus that's turned up in a small number of men who saw duty in Vietnam. It lies dormant in the system, then grows subtly in the tissue until it reaches a point where symptoms appear is if from nowhere.'

'How terrible. I can't believe I haven't heard of it!'

'I gave a lecture on it just last month,' Peck bragged, reaching the door to Murdock's room. 'It will be excerpted in the May issue of the International Review of Medicine. I strongly suggest you read it. In the meantime, let me see to Mr Murdock. If I can get him out of here and to our facilities, I'm expecting a serum to arrive from France by this afternoon and we can begin immediate treatment.'

'Thank God ...'

As Face opened the door and started to enter the room, the nurse began to follow. He stopped abruptly in the doorway and motioned for her to do the same, saying, 'Nurse, I've been immunized against contagion. Hopefully, you've been fortunate enough to avoid contracting anything up to now. Let's not push our luck, okay?'

Blushing the shade of warm beets, the nurse took a step back into the hallway, stammering, 'Y ... yes. Of course, doctor.'

Peck closed the door behind him as he slipped into the room. Howling Mad Murdock was in the far corner, headphones perched upon his head as he hunched over one of the several video games lining the wall. His body twitched and contorted with the intensity of his play, and over the sound effects dispensed by the game, he was singing along to the chorus of 'Satisfaction' in a voice that most closely resembled Tiny Tim on barbiturates.

"cause I tried/and I tried/and I tried/and I tried/I can't get no SATISFACTION!"'

'Murdock!' Peck hissed, coming up behind his entranced companion. But Murdock was too absorbed to hear his name called, and he continued to rock on the heels of his sneakers as he let loose with a bombardment of electronic blips meant to destroy a bevy of hurtling obstacles approaching his spaceship on the video screen.

'"I can't get no/no no no –"'

Face disrupted the proceedings by yanking off Murdock's headphones, along with his black baseball cap. Distracted, Murdock let up his guard long enough for one of the projectiles on the screen to vaporize his spaceship.

'Ah, man!' Murdock whined, wheeling about to face Peck. 'I was practically through that meteor shower. Inter-galactic domination was only moments away!'

There was an almost extra-terrestrial gleam in Murdock's eyes. It was a look he'd mastered over the years, being as it was his meal ticket to free room and board at the hospital, where he was considered to be mentally unhinged as a result of his stint in Vietnam ten years ago. Peck knew better, though, and he waved like a referee for Murdock to ease up with the theatrics.

'C'mon, Murdock. We're going bye-bye,' Face said unfolding the wheelchair propped up against a nearby wall. 'The magic word today is "tuberculosis".'

After retrieving his baseball cap and pulling it down over his receding hairline, Murdock responded to his cue, collapsing into the wheelchair and drawing in a deep breath, then letting it out in the form of a hideous cough that sounded like a diseased trumpet announcing the return of the Black Plague.

'Excellent, Murdock,' Face told him as he began pushing the wheelchair from behind. 'Keep up the good work and we'll be out of here in no time.'

Murdock retorted with another display of simulated consumption as Face reached over his shoulder and threw open the door so he could push his patient out into the hallway. The nurse observed the sudden decline in

Murdock's condition and took a large step back, almost upsetting the hospital cart behind her.

'Oh, no, Mr Murdock,' she gasped, 'How terrible ...'

'It's just a c ... c ... coooaaaaaaroooouuffff!' Murdock almost keeled out of the wheelchair with the force of his coughing fit.

'Not to worry,' Face informed her as he guided Murdock briskly down the corridor. 'If this is just his first day of showing symptoms, as you've suggested, we'll have no trouble saving him, provided we get him to our facilities immediately. I'll need you to sign a release, of course ...'

As Peck held out his clipboard and pointed to the line he wanted the nurse to sign, Murdock coughed once more, then began to moan, 'Ooooooh, doc, I hurt powerfully. I'm not gonna be a goner, am I?'

'No, son. We'll take good care of you,' Face told him. After the nurse signed the release and handed the clipboard back to Peck, they proceeded to the main lobby. Keeping his surgical mask in place, Peck asked the nurse, 'Could you write me up a list of patients Mr Murdock has been in contact with during his stay here?'

'We're fortunate on that front, doctor,' the nurse said. 'He spends most of his time by himself.'

'With my dog, Billy,' Murdock corrected, becoming suddenly frantic. Groping for the nurse's arm, he wailed, 'What about Billy, nurse? He's been in that same position for months!'

The nurse recoiled from Murdock and circled around to the other side of the wheelchair, putting Peck between her and the patient. Face frowned and said, 'Dog? This man has a dog?'

Lowering her voice, the nurse leaned closer to Peck and whispered, 'No, no, you see ... there is no dog ...'

Murdock still managed to overhear her, and his anguish intensified. 'Oh, no, he's gone! We're too late, doc!' He began to sob, but another fit came over him and he rattled off a string of lung-quaking coughs. The nurse couldn't open the main door soon enough.

'Thank you, nurse, you've been most helpful,' Face told

her as he wheeled Murdock out of the building. 'If this man has been eating in the cafeteria, I'd like the dietician's staff to be given full examinations and, if necessary, I'll arrange for shots to be given once I receive more serum from France ... oh, yes ... one of the quirks of this strain is that it only affects males. You needn't worry about yourself being affected. You might be a carrier, though, so I would suggest you up your daily intake of Vitamins C and E. Your chances of transmitting are slim, but every precaution is worth the effort.'

'Of course, doctor,' the nurse replied, visibly relieved.

'My dog Billy!' Murdock cried out again. 'Tell me, he'll make it, doc ...!'

'We'll do the best we can,' Peck told him, trading winks with the nurse.

'Feel better, Mr Murdock,' the nurse called out as Face wheeled his associate down the ramp leading to the walk.

'I feel better already,' Murdock snickered under his breath as he looked up at the blue skies overhead.

'Enjoy it while you can,' Face told him as they headed for the parking lot. 'We've got some nasty business ahead of us ...'

SIX

BA and Hannibal were having only moderate success with their eavesdropping. Once the four SWAT officers had finished changing into their uniforms, they joined a handful of their comrades in going downstairs to the basement firing range for target practice. For close to an hour, BA was forced to tune down the volume on his monitor speaker to keep the constant explosion of bugged gunfire from drawing attention to the parked van. And because there were other men present at the range, the few scraps of conversation BA and Hannibal were able to pick up revealed little new information regarding the contract killing operation.

'Man, I hope this shooting doesn't go on all day, BA grumbled as he reached for the last of the half-dozen donuts he'd bought for breakfast before they'd begun their remote stakeout. 'We need something we can move on.'

'Patience, BA, patience,' Hannibal said, stretching his legs out on the carpeted floor of the van. 'They'll put their popguns away any minute now, then I have a feeling our boys will get some time to themselves.'

'I sure hope so.'

BA polished off the donut and washed it down with a pint of cold milk while Hannibal busied himself with inspecting some of the weapons the A-Team had accumulated in the course of their various scrapes with danger over the years. He was loading bullets into the magazine of an old Browning automatic pistol when there was a sudden knock on the side

44

door of the van.

'What the . . .' BA swiftly reached over and snapped off his equipment, then began covering it with a lightweight sheet of canvas as Hannibal rammed home the magazine in the handle of the automatic and inched toward the door. He was about to peer through a slit in the drawn curtains when a familiar voice sounded outside the van.

'Hannibal? Are you in there? It's me, Maloney.'

'Music to my ears,' Hannibal muttered as he took his finger off the trigger and opened the door. Maloney was in uniform, standing nervously on the grass parkway.

'Mornin', Mr Maloney,' Hannibal greeted him. 'Have any trouble finding us?'

Maloney shook his head. 'You gave me good directions over the phone.'

Gesturing over his shoulder at the equipment BA was putting back into operation, Hannibal said, 'From what we hear, you put on a convincing show for the goon squad.'

Maloney swallowed hard and nodded. 'I think so. I ran into Shaeffer on the way to work and told him I'd decided to keep my mouth shut after all. He seemed to buy it.'

'Yeah, he did,' BA confirmed. 'He told all the other guys you were scared plenty.'

'Well, it wasn't all acting,' Maloney confessed.

'Sorry to make you drive out of your way,' Hannibal said, 'but when I called we hadn't picked up anything over the monitor yet. We just wanted to make sure everything was going according to plan.'

'No problem,' Maloney said. 'Only I gotta get back on the job before I'm missed. I don't want those guys getting suspicious.'

'Don't worry,' Hannibal told him. 'If they start having second thoughts about you, we'll be the first to know. You're in good hands. So is your family.'

'Great. Thanks a lot, guys. I sure do appreciate it.'

'Hey, what did I tell you about thanking us?' Hannibal reminded him with a grin.

'Right.' Maloney snapped off a leisurely salute and walked off to his patrol car, which was parked a few spaces down the street. Hannibal closed the door and set down the Browning as BA turned up the volume on the monitor. There was a mingling of voices and the sound of footsteps echoing off what Hannibal and BA took to be a staircase. It was hard to make out more than a few random words until the four assassins had returned to one of the upper floors and taken refuge in a room. There was the sound of a closing door, then Collins' voice came through loud and clear.

'... you mean I really gotta off this laundry guy?'

Hannibal shot BA a worried glance and Baracus quickly adjusted the control knobs to make the conversation come in even clearer. Collins was still talking, and BA flipped another switch to activate the tape recorder.

'I mean for a puny eight grand? That's only two thou apiece ...'

'Listen to Rockefeller! Two grand is what we each make in a month, Collins!'

Hannibal was straining to follow the discussion. 'I think that was Shaeffer,' he guessed.

'How many more of these do we have to go for?' Collins was wondering aloud. 'I don't know about the rest of you, but ... I mean, I got me a good little stash saved away along with that cabin up by the lake ... I'm about ready to just take it easy and chase some tail for a change. Look, I did this for a little extra dough, and I got it. We all did. Why don't we quit while we're ahead?'

'Because maybe the rest of us aren't as easy to please as you are, Collins.' It was Stark, sounding testy. 'Now, we're going ahead with this hit, got it? And, of course, you know that until we all back out, we're all in. Right?'

There was a moment of silence, during which BA whispered to Hannibal, 'Think they're gonna try something today?'

'Shhhhh,' Hannibal hissed, quieting BA in time for them both to hear the faint sound of a gun's hammer clicking.

'Right, Collins?' Stark was saying coolly.

When Collins' voice came back on over the monitor, it had a weakened edge to it. It was the voice of someone staring down the bore of a .357 Magnum. 'Hey, right ... yeah, of course I know that ... sure, I, ah, was just sayin' ... thinkin' out of turn, that's all, Stark. I got –'

'Zip it, Collins,' Stark ordered. 'Go get on over to Whitsett and Arroyo and dust that laundry guy ... what's his name? Delgado?'

'That's it,' a new voice piped in. It had to be Meadows. 'Can you imagine some guy putting up eight grand to have his brother blown away just so he can take over a stinking laundry? What some people won't do for money, eh?'

There was a burst of sick laughter over the monitor, after which Stark pounded his fist on a desktop and barked, 'Okay, go get it over with!'

As the clandestine gathering was breaking up at the SWAT building, there was a second interruption at the van. While BA was abandoning his equipment in favour of the driver's seat, the side door swung open and Templeton Peck climbed inside, followed by Howling Mad Murdock.

'Hey guys,' Murdock called out happily. 'Long time no see.'

'Not long enough, sucker,' BA growled, stabbing a key into the ignition and firing the engine to life.

'Be nice,' Murdock told him, bringing a fist to his face and coughing into it. 'I've been ill.'

'Not ill enough, either.' BA shifted gears and pulled out into the street, sending the others tumbling in all directions.

'Hey, what's the rush?' Peck asked once he'd regained his balance. 'What's happening?'

'We've got one going down,' Hannibal informed him. 'Our boys are on their way to a hit. Whitsett and Arroyo.'

'Wonderful,' Face groaned. 'They'll be there in half an hour. That doesn't give us much time to lay any groundwork for our battle plan.'

'That depends,' Hannibal said before raising his voice to reach the front seat, 'BA, buy us some time.'

'I'm workin' on it, man,' BA said, screeching rubber as he jockeyed the van through traffic, seeking out the shortest distance between two points.

'And he complains about my flying,' Murdock sniffed, making a face at BA.

47

BA ignored the taunt and whisked the van along at a clip that made the surrounding scenery little more than a blur.

'If we get pulled over, let me do the talking,' Murdock advised.

'We won't get pulled over, man,' BA growled. 'This is Maloney's beat.'

'How nice,' Murdock replied. 'Who's Maloney?'

'Very funny, Murdock,' Face drawled. 'You trying to make it sound like I didn't brief you?'

'Hey, let's knock it off with the intramural squabbles, all right?' Hannibal said, holding onto the nearest armrest for support as BA kept up their accelerated pace.

'Hannibal, what are we gonna do?' Face asked him. 'Even if we catch these guys in the act, we can't place 'em under citizen's arrest. We're wanted by the military, remember? What kind of credibility do you think that'll give us?'

'All I want to do right now is head them off at the pass,' Hannibal said, glancing down at the pistol in his hand. 'If we don't ... well, we can stage a sequel to "Gunfight at the OK Corral".'

BA's efforts proved not to be in vain, as he negotiated a last few hairpin turns and pulled into a back alley just as an elderly man with hunched shoulders was making his way back to the rear entrance to Delgado's House of Laundry, a modest-looking establishment sandwiched among other small businesses. The man was lugging a wastebasket he'd just emptied in the trash bin out back, and he dropped it in shock at the sudden arrival of the van. When Hannibal and Peck bounded out of the vehicle and approached him, the man curled his spindly fingers into puny fists and took a wary step backwards.

'We're not here to hurt you,' Hannibal told the man. 'Are you Senor Delgado?'

'Si, si,' Delgado said, lowering his hands slightly. 'Que pasa?'

'You speak English?' Face asked.

'Si ... yes,' Delgado replied, breaking one fist so that he could stroke the grey wisp of beard on his chin. 'What is it? What is going on?'

'I'm Lieutenant Harve Esterhous and this is my Captain, Roy MacEveety,' Peck explained calmly. 'We're with the Armed Robbery Task Force formed by the Police Commissioner last week. We're trying to crack the ring that's working this area.'

'I have heard nothing about any ring,' Delgado said suspiciously. Noticing that Hannibal was eyeing him intently from head to toe, he straightened his posture and puffed out his chest, making himself look perhaps a year or two younger. 'Besides, I can take care of myself. I am a Delgado!'

BA and Murdock piled out of the van next. As BA backtracked on foot to survey the area, Murdock produced a tape measure from his leather jacket pocket and began measuring Delgado from behind, like a tailor. Delgado waved him away, but Murdock continued to make measurements from a distance, approximating lengths and widths.

'Please, Mr Delgado,' Face continued. 'We need your assistance. We've kept things under wraps so the perpetrators wouldn't know how far along we are in our investigations. They've been hitting small shop owners several times a week, usually just before they open up.'

While Delgado digested this information, BA jogged up to Hannibal and reported, 'They have two good approaches, but the faster escape route's heading east onto Fulton. I figure they'll work it from a rooftop ... either over that movie theatre or the brownstone on the corner.'

Hannibal looked where BA was pointing and nodded, concentrating on a plan that was still taking shape in his mind.

'What does all this have to do with me?' Delgado demanded indignantly.

'One of our sources tells us they're going to hit your laundry shop this morning,' Peck said.

Delgado laughed and a strange twinkle came to his eyes. 'They are? Bueno, bueno!' He rubbed his withered palms together eagerly. 'Let them come. I am armed and ready. I would love to have these pendejos try to take what is mine!'

'Uh, Mr Delgado ... that's not exactly what we had in mind,' Face responded with a sigh.

'It is what I have in mind!' Delgado boasted. 'They think they can do what they want. Well, not to Diego Delgado they cannot! I will grind the filthy cabrones –'

The elderly man's soliloquy was interrupted by a firm fist that came crashing into the side of his face with a force that crumpled him to the pavement. Face moaned as he rubbed his bruised knuckles, then helped Hannibal pick Delgado up by the armpits.

'I sure hated to do that, but we didn't have time for a debate.'

'I'm sure he thanks you from he bottom of his heart,' Hannibal told Peck. 'Now let's get busy ...'

SEVEN

A nearby church tower was emitting nine chimes from its programmed bells when the folding steel gate across the entrance to Delgado's House of Laundry began to creak open. The stoop-shouldered proprietor compressed the gate into a recessed cavity, then wheeled out a large antique washtub bearing a bright flag that read 'OPEN FOR BUSI—NESS'. The street was still deserted, though, and the only person who seemed to notice the old man going through his daily routine was Al Collins, who was lining Delgado up on the sights of his high-powered rifle. Still in uniform, Collins was poised on the rooftop of the corner hardware store, two buildings away from the laundry. Even an amateur would have had trouble missing at that range.

Keeping his rifle in place, Collins drew up his walkie-talkie and whispered into it, 'Okay, I've got a bead on him.'

There was a slight crackle over the communicator, followed by Meadows' voice, telling Collins, 'Then what are you waiting for? Waste him before the street gets crowded.'

Down below, the old man chained the antique washer to the foundation of the building, then paused to massage a kink in his lower back before heading inside. He never made it. As he was taking his first step towards the doorway, a gunshot ripped through the morning air and ploughed into Delgado's back, right between his shoulder blades. The impact was sufficient to spin the old man completely around before he sprawled face-first onto the sidewalk.

51

Atop the House of Laundry, Templeton Peck was crouched alongside an air-conditioning unit. He had a walkie-talkie of his own, and he raised it to his lips without taking his eyes off the binoculars he had trained on the hardware store.

'Muzzle flash from the three storey brick job on the corner,' he spat into the mouthpiece as he swung the binoculars down to ground level. 'And I've got a definite someone laying low on the front seat of a grey four-door parked at the corner. Gonna make their exit east bound, just like you figured ...'

As Face watched on through the binoculars, Collins suddenly cleared the last rung of the brownstone's fire escape and bolted across the sidewalk to the grey sedan, yanking the back door open and lunging inside. Adam Meadows sprang up behind the wheel and put the car in gear, rolling out into the street as Collins slapped him on the shoulder. Face saw it all and smirked to himself, 'Enjoy it while you can, boys, 'cause it ain't gonna last ...'

Sure enough, before the sedan was even halfway down the block, the A-Team van roared out into the street from a side alley and headed straight for Meadows and Collins. The two vehicles were converging on a collision course when both drivers jerked hard on their steering wheels, trying to veer out of each other's way. BA was able to bound his van up onto the sidewalk a few yards before coasting to a halt back on the street, but Meadows lost control of the sedan, spinning out wildly. A fire hydrant and telephone pole bore the brunt of the wipeout, stopping the sedan before it could plough into any buildings. BA turned the van around and headed back to the wreckage as Meadows and Collins were prying their way out into the open. Collins saw the approaching van and reached to his hip for his service revolver. Before he could draw aim on BA, though, he was startled by a voice behind him.

'Don't try it, pal!'

It was Face, peering around the corner of the laundry shop, exposing just enough of his binoculars to give the impression that he was armed.

Collins fell for the bluff and rushed for the cover of the front doorway of the laundry shop, sidestepping the body on the sidewalk. Meadows hid behind the crumpled front end of the sedan and fired off three shots in Face's direction, scarring the cinderblock of the building but missing their mark.

'Take him from the right!' Meadows told Collins before turning his attention back to the nearby van.

Collins nodded and crouched low as he began creeping along the front of the laundry, nearing the alley where Face was hiding. As he passed his sniping victim, however, the would-be corpse suddenly spun upright and planted the tip of a Browning automatic into Collins' ribcage. It was Hannibal.

'Freeze, hotshot,' Smith advised the SWAT man.

Meadows caught the action out of the corner of his eye, but by the time he could draw aim, Hannibal was on his feet and was using Collins as a human shield.

'Party's over,' Hannibal shouted to Meadows. 'Be a nice boy and drop your gun.'

Meadows kept his Magnum pointed at the chest of his partner, but refrained from shooting. Sweating with fear, Collins told him, 'You heard him. Come on, Meadows, drop it ... hey, do it already ... quit pointing that thing at me!'

'Listen to your buddy,' Hannibal advised Meadows, staying behind Collins.

While Meadows was preoccupied with Hannibal and Collins, Howling Mad Murdock quietly slipped out the rear of the van, cradling a Thompson submachine gun in his arms. He took a deep breath, then jumped out into the open and let the gun start talking. A spray of bullets danced close to Meadows, catching him off guard. Leaping reflexively to one side, the officer rammed loudly into the unseen telephone pole. With a groan of pain, he dropped his gun and fell off balance to the ground. Murdock rushed forward and kicked the Magnum out of Meadows' reach. Grinning at the downed officer, Murdock told him, 'I'm conducting field research for the No Sweat Underarm Deodorant company. Would you be so kind as to show me your armpits?'

'What?' Meadows blabbered incredulously.

'Put your hands up, fool,' BA translated, getting out of the van and coming over.

As Face joined the others and frisked Collins for other weapons, he told Hannibal, 'Nice performance, Hannibal. You had me there for a minute. I thought the bullet-proof vest didn't work.'

'I'm just glad I decided to wear two and put one on backwards,' Hannibal said, shoving Collins over next to Meadows. 'Just like these slimes to try to nail someone in the back.'

'Who are you guys?' Meadows asked sullenly as the A-Team headed back to the van, richer by two Magnums and a high-powered rifle. While the others piled into the van, Hannibal paused on the street and told the assassins, 'We're the guys who are gonna run you off the road. You got it? You're shut down. Take it back to Stark. You're all measured for body bags. We hear about you planning another hit and you'll be tryin' 'em on for size at the county morgue.'

Hannibal hopped into the van and BA floored it. The A-Team roared off down the road just as the first flow of morning traffic began creeping into the area.

'Who are those guys?' Meadows wondered again.

'Beats me,' Collins said. 'All I know is you're gonna be the one who explains this to Stark.'

'Me? Why me?'

'Hey, I held up my end of things,' Collins defended himself. 'If you wouldn't have wrecked the car, we'd have been outta here.'

'Right, and what about when the real Delgado turns up alive when you say you plugged him?' Meadows complained.

'Aw, the hell with it. Let's just get out of here.'

A third time Meadows pondered the question of the day. 'Who were those guys?'

EIGHT

'Who the hell do you *think* they were?'

Dolph Stark bombarded his coffee with sugar cubes and stirred them into oblivion before taking a sip. He was in a venemous mood, and his three partners were all edgy, each one hoping they wouldn't be the next one targeted for Stark's invective. They were holding down a back booth at one of the many restaurants around town that offered discount rates to any kind of cop that walked in the door as a hedge against robbers or other rabble that might disrupt business.

'Cops maybe?' Richard Shaeffer guessed. 'Could be some guys from another division caught wind of us.'

'Nah, no way,' Collins argued. 'These guys didn't act like no cops.'

'They're pros, Captain,' Meadows said, dunking his Danish. 'And they nailed us dead bang . . .'

Stark let out an irritated sigh and plopped still another cube into his drink. 'I can't leave anything in your hands, can I? I have to come along to make sure things go right, is that it?'

'We were outnumbered,' Collins blurted out defensively. He was going to dish out more excuses, but a glance at Stark told him the Captain wasn't interested in alibis. Turning his gaze down to his plate, Collins dabbed at the last of his hashed browns as he mumbled, 'I knew we were pushing it on this last one. Someone had to find out sooner or later . . .'

'It had to be Maloney,' Stark surmised. 'I figured a threat would've kept that plate of jello on hold. We told him what would happen if he yelled fire. Damn it, we should have dusted him in the first place!'

'But what if he has some papers stashed around somewhere with our names on it?' Collins asked. 'If he goes belly up and we get linked to it, we're lookin' at a quick ride to Death Row. And, besides, we don't know for a fact that he's the one who blew the whistle on us.'

'I think the Captain's right,' Meadows said. 'Instead of going to Metcalf, Maloney hired out the local Seven Samurai instead. That's what makes sense to me.'

'But how did they find out about the Delgado hit?' Shaeffer said. 'No way Maloney could have even known about that. No way.'

Stark downed half his coffee, thinking things through. He finally decided, 'They had an ear on us.'

'A bug?' Meadows said. 'You think they had us bugged?'

Once his cup was emptied, Stark nodded briskly. Caffeine and sugar rattled through his system, tensing his already taut nerves. 'I don't want any more talk around the room at headquarters until we sweep it for mikes.' Pounding his fist on the table with frustration, he swore, 'Who the hell were those guys?'

Those guys were huddled in BA's van, which was discreetly parked in a back alley a few blocks away, out of view of the main roads. BA had the equipment working again, but on Hannibal's signal he turned off the monitor, leaving the reel-to-reel running to record the conversation still taking place back at the coffee shop.

'We've primed the pump,' Hannibal announced to the others. 'Now let's see if we can't kick it over.'

'Sounds like fun,' Murdock ventured, glancing up from the comic book he'd been reading intently. 'That was my favourite game as a kid. Kick the pump . . . ah, the memories, livin' next door to the filling station –'

'Shut up, you crazy fool!' BA snapped, silencing Murdock momentarily. He then looked back at Hannibal and said, 'I still don't know why you went and had us send 'em that warning, man. We shoulda put 'em on ice when we had 'em redhanded.'

Hannibal grinned around his cigar and reflected, 'I call that style.'

'I call that dumb,' BA said, 'You don't kick a snake when you're trying to sneak up on it.'

'Well, maybe I got carried away with the drama of the moment,' Hannibal conceded. 'But, in the long run, it'll work in our favour. It's all part of my plan.'

'Plan?' Murdock cried out. 'I didn't hear any plan.' Pounding his head like someone trying to get rid of water in the ear, he rambled on, 'I must be fading in and out again.'

'Not this time,' Face told him. Smiling blandly at Hannibal, he said, 'If you have a plan, perhaps you'd care to share it with us? I'd hate to miss my cue.'

Hannibal took the cigar from his lips and fingered it as he spoke, staring into the smoke. 'They've got to have an Achilles heel. We'll keep pushing these guys ... and pushing ... and pushing ... until we find their weak link. Same kind of tactics we used to nail that Cong general and his men in Khe San. Remember that one?'

'The one where I took it in the leg?' Face asked.

'And I got shot down?' Murdock put in.

Swatting away the smoke that had drifted his way, BA groused, 'Man, that was a *terrible* plan!'

Hannibal shrugged, popping the cigar back into his mouth and puffing it back to life. 'By now we should have the kinks worked out of it, right?'

'If you say so, Hannibal,' Face said uncertainly. 'What's our next step then?'

Hannibal checked his pockets, then asked, 'Anybody got a dime?'

A long-legged, short-haired waitress with deep blue eyes that could melt a man's heart and pants at the same time drifted over to the booth where the SWAT officers were seated. As she started refilling coffees, she said, 'Captain Stark? Phone call for you ...'

Sliding his way out of the booth, Stark told the men, 'I left word with the watch commander we'd be here. Get ready, we may be rolling.'

As Stark strode off to answer the phone, Collins ogled the waitress, baring a predatory grin. 'Hey, babe, how's it going?'

'Fine,' the waitress responded nonchalantly. 'Is there anything else you'd like?'

Arching an eyebrow, Collins cooed, 'Anything else I could possibly like ... you got.'

'My, how original,' she gushed back sarcastically. 'You could give lessons.'

'Ouch!' Meadows winced, trying to hold back his laughter as the waitress wandered off to attend to other customers. 'The ladies' man gets shot down in flames!'

'Ah, what are you talking about?' Collins jeered. 'I tell ya, she's in love with me. No way around it.'

As Meadows and Shaeffer continued to razz Collins, Stark reached the phone and picked up the receiver.

'Stark here.'

The voice that came on over the other line wasn't that of the watch commander. It was Hannibal. 'Meadows is right, Cap. We're pros ... and you guys are scuzzballs.'

Stark cupped his hand over the mouthpiece and quickly scanned the inside of the restaurant. The lunch rush was still a half-hour away, so there were only a few other people dining, and none of them looked suspicious. Taking his hand away from the receiver, he huffed, 'I don't know who or what your story is, Jack, but you happen to be talking to a cop.'

'Oh, is that a fact? Funny, none of the cops I know sit around over coffee and talk about an unsuccessful murder they attempted that morning.'

'Hey, who the hell is this?'

The only answer Stark received was the clicking of Hannibal hanging up the phone, followed by the monotonous drone of the dial tone. Stark hung up on his end, grinding his jaws with growing fury. Storming back to the booth, he seethed, 'Get outta those seats, right now!'

Dropping the smirks from their faces, Meadows, Shaeffer and Collins quickly slid out of the booth and stood by watching as Stark dropped to his knees and peered under the table. There were a few dozen hardened globs of gum hanging from the underside like dwarf stalactites, but he could find no trace of a remote microphone. As he shifted his attention to the cushioned seats, the other officers exchanged wary looks.

'What's up, Captain?' Meadows asked him. 'You lose something? We can lend a hand looking if you want ...'

Ignoring the offer, Stark finished frisking the seats and stood upright to check the light hovering over the table. Still no luck.

'Damn them!' he cursed, resorting to one of his patented fist-slams on the tabletop. 'How did they know?'

'Was that them on the phone?' Shaeffer wondered.

'Damn them!' Stark repeated, drawing stares from the other customers. Heading for the door, he ordered his underlings, 'Let's get out of here!'

'You bet, Captain,' Shaeffer said as Collins and Meadows fell in step behind him so that the four of them were taking long, purposeful strides like Gestapo agents on the way to Anne Frank's hideout.

'But how could they have bugged us in there?' Collins said once they were outside. 'I mean ... in a coffee shop?'

The rumpled sedan was parked just outside the door. Stark made a face as he surveyed the damage for the second time, now associating it with the taunting voice he'd heard on the phone. Letting out a long breath, he brought himself under control and informed his colleagues, 'These guys know exactly what game they're playing. All we gotta do is get on the board and then we'll turn this around.'

'I sure hope so,' Collins said.

Stark's car was next to the sedan. As he was getting into it, he said, 'I'll be at Brenda's in case they contact one of you.'

Shaeffer nodded. Collins and Meadows stood with him and they watched as Stark drove out of the parking lot, then headed into their own battered vehicle.

'He get's bent out of shape, so he takes some time out to party with some skirt,' Collins complained. 'Must be nice. I don't know about you guys, but I'm getting real tired of nosing up to him all the time.'

'You got a bad attitude, Collins, that's your problem,' Shaeffer told him.

'Bugging the coffee shop like that ... they must have known we go there all the time,' Meadows deduced. 'Who are these guys, man?'

'We're the eighties' answer to the Fantastic Four!' Murdock whooped at the monitor speaker inside the van as he tossed aside his comic book. 'That's who we are!'

'Easy, Murdock, easy,' Hannibal said as he climbed back into the van.

'Good goin', Hannibal,' BA said from behind the wheel. 'You put a nice bee in that Stark dude's bonnet.'

'Thank you, BA,' Hannibal said, settling down in the front passenger seat. 'Now for our next step. I think I saw a florist shop a block back. Let's hit it.'

While BA backtracked to the desired location, Hannibal quickly sketched out his plan to the others. When he finished, Face laughed lightly and held a palm out for Hannibal to slap, telling him, 'I gotta hand it to ya, Hannibal. You know how to antagonize someone.'

'Aw, shucks, it's just a little knack I picked up in my youth.'

There was a parking space directly in front of the florist shop. BA left the van running and stayed put in the driver's seat as Murdock hopped out the side door. Hannibal peeled a few bills from his wallet and handed them out the window to Murdock. 'You know what I want. Something tasteful.'

'Perhaps with some red roses in it?' Murdock suggested snootily. 'The rose, after all, is a passion flower, that –'

'Murdock!' BA warned, 'Just go and do it, fool!'

Murdock took a step back and slipped into the role of shrink, reminding BA, 'You should take care to watch your attitude when speaking to people with fragile psyches. You give the impression that your attitude is singularly and pointedly directed at the individual, when really you're just one mean, angry sucker to everybody.'

BA pointed one ring-encrusted finger at the florist shop

and closed the other into a fist as he glared at Murdock. 'Git!'

'Gone,' Murdock replied, turning heel and bounding towards the shop entrance.

'Really, BA, you shouldn't treat Murdock like that,' Face called out from the back of the van, where he was trying to work the controls of the eavesdropping equipment. 'You're gonna drive him nuts!'

'That fool's already there,' BA retorted. 'He's just trying to make me that way so he can have some company!'

NINE

Brenda Webb wasn't related to Jack, not by a long shot. Her bloodlines looked like they had more in common with Dolly Parton and Bo Derek. A voluptuous woman with a swirling mass of blonde curls surrounding her soft features, she made her living by donning vibrant shades of lipstick and blowing kisses at fashion photographers who helped spread her face across the pages of a dozen women's magazines. She lived in a posh condominium on the beach and counted Dolph Stark as just one of her many boyfriends. Since Dolph wasn't the type to seek out exclusive relationships, he had no qualms about having to share Brenda with others. If he was looking for companionship and she wasn't available, he knew half a dozen ladies prowling Hollywood Boulevard that would be more than willing to show him a good time. Brenda, though, dispensed her charms and favours for free. And, being as this was Wednesday afternoon, Stark showed up at Brenda's condo prepared for his most coveted moments of the week, an hour of nonstop massage, followed by whatever came naturally.

Brenda greeted Stark in a pair of cutoff jogging pants and a baseball jersey that hid little of her anatomical virtues. Offering him a light kiss, she said, 'So how's my big bruiser?'

'Lousy,' Stark said, striding into the room and quickly peeling off his gun belt. Fully clothed, he dived headfirst onto the bed, letting out a miserable groan. 'I need some magic fingers real bad.'

'Coming right up,' Brenda said sprightly, joining Stark on the bed and straddling his lower back. Her hands lighted on the officer's shoulders and started kneading at the flesh beneath his shirt like twin spiders frolicking on a trampoline. She found resistance, though. Stark's muscles were as taut and tense as his nerves. 'Dolph, I've never seen you this tense,' she told him, trying to loosen him up. 'Something at work?'

'Yeah,' Stark said gruffly. 'Yeah, something at work. Whaddya think?'

'Whoah, boy,' Brenda told him. 'I'm on your side, remember?'

'Sorry.'

'Listen, why don't you take your shirt off so I can do a better job, okay?' Brenda climbed off Stark and gave him a playful swat on the seat of his pants.

'Maybe you're right.' Stark sat up in bed and started unfastening the top buttons of his shirt. 'You got something cold with a little kick to it? That might help, too.'

'Sure thing. I've got all kinds of imported beers from –'

Brenda was cut short by the chiming of the front doorbell. As she went to answer it, Stark quickly buttoned his shirt back up and leaned forward on the bed so that his hand fell upon the butt on his pistol. 'You expecting anyone?' he asked Brenda.

'No ... not really.' The front door was in the hallway just outside the bedroom, and as she reached for the deadbolt, Brenda called out, 'Who is it?'

'Florist.'

'Flowers?' Brenda said, unlocking the door. Glancing back at Stark, she chuckled, 'I hope they're from you, or else I'm going to have some awkward explaining to do.'

Stark put his gunbelt back on as he joined Brenda in the hallway. She opened the door, revealing a massive, self-standing floral wreath adorned with a satin banner that read 'RIP'. Howling Mad Murdock was standing behind the display with paper wings stapled on his ball cap so that he looked like some crazy aberration of the FTD Mercury mascot.

'"Rest In Peace"?' Brenda exclaimed. 'I think you have the wrong place, friend.'

Murdock checked the number on the door and shook his head. 'No, Ma'am. This here's the place. There's more, too.' Murdock was wearing a portable cassette player on his belt, and he hummed a few bars to make sure his voice was in key before lapsing into a song-and-dance routine, performed to the tune of an old sixties classic, 'Snoopy vs. the Red Baron'. Murdock's was an interpretive dance, approximating a marionette in the hands of a drunk.

> '"*Now Snoopy had swore that he'd*
> *get that man*
> *So he asked the Great Pumpkin for*
> *a new battle plan.*
> *While the Baron was laughin'*
> *He got him in his sight*
> *Ten, twenty, thirty, forty, fifty –*"'

'Hey, knock it off all ready!' Stark interrupted brusquely as he pushed past Brenda and toppled the wreath. 'Who sent this? Huh? I want answers, chump!'

Murdock turned off his cassette and shrank back in the face of Stark's wrath. 'Hey, look, I'm just a driver, know what I mean?' he babbled. 'I'm not even supposed to sing, but the Chiquita banana got held up at Valley Presbyterian.'

'Enough!' Stark roared, pointing down the outside hallway to the stairs. 'Take a hike, and tell whoever sent you that it's gonna take more than flowers and a clown show to unnerve Dolph Stark.'

'What about the song?' Murdock protested weakly. 'You still have two more verses coming.'

Stark slammed the door on Murdock and charged past Brenda into her kitchen, helping himself to a beer from the refrigerator. Ripping off the pull tab, he took a long drink and went back into the bedroom, where he began pacing. Brenda watched him, disconcerted.

'Hey, Dolph, take it easy, huh? I'm sure it was a screw-up at the flower shop. That's all. It was just a mistake somebody made.'

'You're right there.' Stark drained the beer and crushed the can in his fist before tossing it into a nearby wastebasket. 'Somebody made a big mistake. A real big one.'

'Dolph, honey, sit down.' Brenda stepped forward and eased Stark onto the edge of the bed. He sat upright, still stewing in the juice of his anger. Brenda knelt on the bed behind him and began stroking his shoulders again. 'Come on, now . . . relax,' she urged him. 'You've been real on edge.'

Brenda nuzzled her lips against Stark's neck, leaving a trail of kisses as she worked her way around to his chin. Stark's resistance began to fade, especially when Brenda began to purr. It was a soft, seductive purr, so soft that it was barely picked up by the transmitter housed in the collar button of Stark's shirt . . .

'Oh oh, sounds like romance time,' Face said, listening to the bedroom sounds coming over the monitor speaker in the van. Hannibal and BA were there with him, stifling smirks of laughter. The next few sounds to be heard by the eavesdroppers were those of rustling clothes and more purring. Stark and Brenda were doing a duet.

'You know, Dolphin, you haven't told me you love me in days,' Brenda was whispering suggestively.

BA whistled lowly and shook his head to himself. Hannibal's smile widened as he suddenly shifted position and pulled a handful of change from his pants pocket. Finding a dime, he held it up as if it were the Hope Diamond. As he reached for the door to let himself out of the van, Face grabbed him by the wrist and said, 'Aw, come on, Hannibal . . . you wouldn't. Not now . . .'

'We'll see about that.' Before Hannibal could let himself out, though, the van door opened and Murdock climbed in.

'You should have seen me, guys,' he bragged. 'Fred Astaire's got nothing on me.'

'Fred Astaire's almost ninety years old, Murdock,' Face retorted.

'Excuse me,' Hannibal told Murdock, clutching his dime as he left the van. Murdock watched him curiously, then looked to Face and BA.

'What's up with Hannibal?'

'He's on the jazz, man,' BA chortled. 'Hannibal's on the jazz.'

Before closing the door on his friends, Hannibal laughed, 'I can't help it. I eat this stuff up with a spoon.'

Stark was ready to graduate from purring to a more demonstrative form of communication. After tossing his gunbelt over the headboard, he began unbuttoning his shirt once again, singing a snatch of an old Bee Gees song. 'How deep is your lah-ah-ah-ah-ah-ah-ahve?'

'Deep enough for you, darlin',' Brenda promised him, squirming across the bed toward him. She was about to help him out of his shirt when the phone rang.

'My God, it's a conspiracy!' Brenda joked. 'Well, I'm not home ...'

Stark wasn't quite as ready to shake off the interruption. 'Answer it,' he told Brenda.

'Forget it,' she replied, taking a pillow and trying to muffle the persistent ringing. Stark leaned over, however, and swatted the pillow aside. Picking up the receiver, he covered the mouthpiece and handed it to Brenda.

'I want you to answer it.'

'Party pooper,' Brenda teased, taking the phone. 'Hello? ... yes, he's here ...'

She gave the phone back to Stark, shrugging her shoulders.

'I know who it is.' Stark howled into the receiver, 'What is it this time?'

'Hey, Captain, I hope I haven't pulled you away from anything important.'

'How long you wanna play this game?' Stark asked Hannibal. 'Huh? How long you gonna hide at the other end of a receiver? I want a meet. You and me. Tonight.'

'Got a favourite place you like? Maybe where you bury the bodies or something?'

Stark thought it over a moment, then said, 'Indian Dunes. Four miles from the exit. At eleven. Alone.'

'See you then,' Hannibal told him. 'Oh, one other thing. If

you don't mind my giving a bit of advice. You really should tell them you love them every couple days ... bye!'

Stark looked as if he were ready to demolish the phone with the same force he'd used on the beer can. He slammed the receiver down and stared wildly into space. The cords on his neck rose to the surface and his face flushed red.

'Hey, Dolph, what is it?' Brenda asked. 'You look kinda spooky, kid.'

But he wasn't paying attention to her. Inner turmoil held him in a maddened trance. Standing up, he grabbed his gunbelt and slung it around his waist on the way to the door. Brenda didn't try to stop him.

TEN

Amy Allen was working overtime at the paper, as usual. After providing the A-Team with Brenda Webb's address, she'd gone back to work revising her notes on a feature story she was working on about ways in which crime elements were filtering gambling and prostitution operations across the Nevada border into small California towns a few miles in from the state line. Of particular interest to her was a rundown mobile home park located just outside Bad Rock, where half the trailers supposedly served as bordellos or gaming houses run by organized crime. Her contact on the story was Simon Commonble, an old college friend who was now a private investigator specializing in missing person cases. He'd been trying to track down a missing teenage girl for a Paso Robles couple when the trail led him to Bad Rock. After a few weeks of snooping around, he'd found the girl working at one of the trailers and convinced her to return home. Commonble, however, had retained an interest in Bad Rock and continued to spend time there, trying to track down the identities of other young women working at the trailers of ill repute in the hopes that he could then get in touch with their parents and secure a commission for having found their daughters. Far from an altruistic motive, granted, but Commonble figured he was performing a worthwhile service and had no qualms about seeking payment for his troubles. He'd run into Amy one day while they were both at the County Courthouse in LA looking over records, and after catching wind of Commonble's doings, Amy'd started working on her story. That was more than a month ago, and she was still trying to get a handle on the whole sordid enterprise, having made a few trips to Bad Rock herself to check things out.

As the sun was dipping behind the urban landscape outside her office window, Amy clicked off her word processor and rubbed her tired eyes. She'd been at her desk for close to eight hours now, and the stiffness in her lower back was becoming unbearable. After calling it a day, she left her office and stopped off at the vending machines down the hall for a few quarters' worth of supper. Hannibal had dropped by an hour before to tell her the A-Team was parked down in the underground garage while BA made some modifications of the van, but she'd been on the phone with Commonble at the time and hadn't pressed for details. She decided to take her Twinkies and Mountain Dew down to the basement to find out what was going on with the SWAT mission and why BA was tinkering with the van.

There were only a few cars parked in the underground garage. The black van was half-hidden in a concrete alcove behind the elevators, where Amy found BA dilligently at work on the vehicle's front end, replacing one set of headlights with another, odder-looking pair.

'So what's happening?' Amy asked BA. 'Why the light switch?'

'Can't send a boy out to do a man's job,' BA replied cryptically, without taking his eyes off his work.

Before Amy could ask for a more coherent explanation, Hannibal said, 'How's your story coming?'

'Great,' Amy said. 'Commonble's onto something big, he tells me. He's off to some sort of secret rendezvous that he thinks will break the case. I should hear about it tomorrow.'

The side door of the van swung open while Amy was speaking and Face climbed out, followed by Murdock, who informed Hannibal, 'Stark just contacted the last of the othes. He's still at the restaurant down the street, but he said he'll be moving out shortly.'

Face shook his head, muttering, 'I sure didn't think we'd

get away with those buttons as long as we have.'

'They'll think of it sooner or later,' Hannibal said. 'When they do, we've lost our advantage.'

'I've been at a disadvantage all my life,' Murdock claimed. 'You get used to it.'

BA grunted as he tightened one last nut, then stood up and wiped his hands off on a dirty rag, announcing, 'All ready.'

'Is it going to work, BA?' Hannibal asked.

'My part of the plan always works.'

'Good, then let's head 'em up and move 'em out,' Hannibal ordered, moving around to the passenger's side of the van. Smiling at Amy, he added, 'Catch you later, kiddo.'

'What do you mean? I want to come along.'

'Not for this,' Face told her.

'Now, just a minute,' Amy said firmly. 'I'm part of this team, too.'

Hannibal pointed at her and said, 'Then you'll take orders when they're given. We're going to Indian Dunes. If we're not in touch with you by midnight, call Maloney and the feds, okay?'

Amy crossed her arms, jutting her lower lip out in a gesture of petulance. 'I appreciate the concern, but I can take care of myself, you know. I've done it in –'

'Amy,' Hannibal cut in, 'I happen to be concerned with everyone here. Tonight's gonna get heavy-duty. Combat situation. We've been there, so we know what we're up against and what we have to do. Having someone along who doesn't have that kind of experience is dangerous for everyone. This has nothing to do with chauvinism, and you know it.'

'Okay, okay,' Amy conceded. 'I see your point.'

'Good.' Now in his seat, Hannibal looked over at BA. 'Let's hit it.'

As the van engine started up, Amy took a step back and called out, 'Hannibal . . . you know these guys aren't the type who go down easily. What happens if you can't get them to confess?'

'It's too soon to think about that. My plans roll one step at a time.'

'Good luck,' Amy said with a wave as the van backed out of its space and headed for the exit. 'Be careful.'

Once the van was gone from view, Amy took a thoughtful bite from her Twinkie and washed it down with some of the soda, then headed for her car, trying to assure herself that the A-Team would live up to its reputation and land on its feet at the end of its upcoming confrontation. Nonetheless, worry wormed its way through her, and as she left the garage, she couldn't help but feel concern for the men's fate ...

ELEVEN

The dunes were dark and silent. Scattered bits of hearty vegetation rose defiantly from the sand, which extended out from the main road in a series of rolling hills, looking like the folds of some gigantic brain. Overhead a thin wedge of moon sliced through thin clouds skimming in from the coast. There was an aura of brooding desolation in the air, but the relative silence was soon ruptured by the throaty roar of a truck as it sped into the parking lot and past the partition that led to the sands. The vehicle was equipped to handle rugged terrain, and with a grinding of gears it scaled the first slope of the dunes effortlessly and then proceeded across the sifting sands until it reached a clearing flanked on one side by a high-pitched rise and on the other by the sheer facing of basalt cliffs pocked with caves.

Adam Meadows was at the wheel, chewing voraciously on a toothpick to work off tension. 'This the place?' he asked Stark, who was sitting next to him, his gun already out.

Stark nodded as he got out of the truck and moved around back to open the rear doors. Collins and Shaeffer scrambled out, each man carrying a walkie-talkie and high-powered rifle with scope sights. Because he was familiar with the area, Stark didn't have to waste time plotting strategy. Pointing to various locations surrounding the clearing, he commanded, 'Collins, you take that ridge over to the right . . . the same one we used last time. Shaeffer, up along that slope near the caves. I want the whole quadrant covered in case they try to send a man out around back.'

'Righto,' Collins said, starting out. Shaeffer strode through the sand in the opposite direction.

'And remember,' Stark called out after them, 'This is it. As soon as we determine how many there are, Meadows'll give the signal and it goes down.'

'Don't worry,' Collins shouted back over his shoulder, 'when we drive out of here tonight, those slimeballs will be lunch for the sand flies.'

They'd arrived early to set up their positions, and by the time eleven o'clock rolled around, Meadows had gone through enough toothpicks to make a baseball bat, but his nerves were still on end.

'Where the hell are they?' he snapped anxiously as he shifted in the driver's seat.

'They'll show up, don't worry,' Stark said calmly. Meadows had turned the truck around since their arrival, and both men stared out the front windshield at the tracks they'd made earlier.

'I'd feel a lot better about this if I knew who they –'

'Quiet!' Stark suddenly cried out, holding a hand up to silence Meadows. 'I think I hear them coming!'

The windows of the truck were open, and soon a faint drone grew in intensity, taking on the unmistakable sound of a labouring engine. Moments later, the dark outline of the A-Team van came into view, following the twin indentations in the sand the SWAT truck had left.

'Driving with no headlights,' Stark mused. 'These guys know what they're doing, all right.' Stroking the tip of his pistol against his chin, he allowed himself a grin of anticipation, 'Oh, this should be good.'

'I'm glad you're *looking* forward to it,' Meadows said. 'Me, I'd just as soon have met them ... YEEEEOWWWW!'

Meadow's cry was brought on by the sudden flashing of the other vehicle's headlights. The two beams of light were so incredibly fierce in their brightness that both Stark and Meadows were temporarily blinded, having covered their eyes against the glare too late. Even after he blinked his eyes several times, Stark's vision was still obscured by the afterimage of the headlights.

'Damn those bastards, they'll pay for this!' he seethed.

Across the way, Hannibal smirked inside the van and reached for the microphone of a police radio that had come into their hands during a previous caper. 'Watch your tongue, Captain,' he baited. 'Hows about tuning in to channel 38, tack two, so we can have a chat, eh?'

As they waited for a response, Hannibal and BA traded glances. BA pointed out the window at his handiwork, saying, 'See, Hannibal, I told you my part of the plan always works. Unless those suckers were wearing shades they ain't seein' so good right now.'

'You done good, kid,' Hannibal told him, just as Stark's voice crackled over both the radio and the monitor speaker in the back of the van.

'Stark here.'

'Care to step out and talk, Captain?' Hannibal asked.

'Yeah, sure,' Stark snorted. 'Then maybe you pump a couple rounds into my breadbasket. How about you first?'

'Ready or not, here I come.' Hannibal put the microphone back and opened his door. BA reached out and grabbed him by the shirt sleeve.

'What if they got a surprise we don't know about, man? You can't go out there.'

'Don't be a spoilsport, BA.' Hannibal removed BA's hand from his shirt and stepped out into the night.

'Fool's on the jazz,' BA mumbled under his breath, staying put. 'On the jazz . . .'

Hannibal stepped down onto the sand and slammed the door hard so they could hear him in the truck. Stepping around in front of the van, he almost disappeared from view between the headlights as he shouted out, 'Your turn. Come on, Stark, let's see a little moxie!'

There was no reaction at first from the truck, then Stark cautiously eased out, squinting as he held one hand out before his face to help filter the glare shining his way. He took up a similar position to Hannibal in front of the SWAT truck as Meadows turned on their headlights, which paled in comparison to those of the van.

'You've been jerking my chain for two days now,' Stark told Hannibal. 'What is it you're after, huh?'

'Simple. I'm offering you a chance to live,' Hannibal explained. 'Tomorrow moring the four of you march into the Police Commissioner's office and turn yourselves in for all the murders you've been paid to commit.'

Stark laughed loudly and spat in the sand. 'You think a couple phone calls and a wreath of flowers are gonna make me want to send myself up for life?'

'It's either that or the death penalty, Stark,' Hannibal warned him. 'And that's already been passed. By me. You only get this one chance at a reprieve.'

'I've passed a few sentences myself.'

Hannibal paused to light a cigar, then said, 'If you want, have Meadows ring up your sentries and see if they found anything nice out there in the night air.'

Inside his truck, Meadows squrimed at the mention of his name. His eyesight was starting to come back, but he still had to grope along the dashboard to get his hands on the walkie-talkie next to him. 'Collins!' he howled, 'Show this gonzo we mean business!'

Seconds later, a figure rose into view atop the nearby ridge and raised a rifle to his shoulder. Two shots were fired off in quick succession, but neither one of them came close to hitting Hannibal. One pierced the front end of the SWAT truck, knocking out one of the headlights and forcing Stark to dive face-first into the sand. The second taught the windshield how to impersonate a spiderweb, zipping through the glass and imbedding itself in the passenger seat next to Meadows.

Up on the ridge top, Templeton Peck lowered the rifle and clucked his tongue as he looked over at Collins, who was writhing in the sand, struggling at his binds like a losing contestant at a Houdini festival. 'Rifle pulls to the left,' Peck told him. 'Your Captain almost lost a vital piece of equipment.'

Collins said something through his gag, and although it was incoherent, Face got the message. 'Behave yourself, Collins. Be a shame if I had to leave you for the sand flies . . .

now where have I heard that line before?'

Down by the riddled truck, Meadows was crawling out into the open, clutching desperately to his walkie-talkie as he looked to the cliffs for deliverance, gasping, 'Richie! Shaeffer, are you there? Come in, damn it!' Punching in the receiver button, Meadows was treated to the muffled sounds of rock and roll music instead of a confirmation from Shaeffer. As Meadows stared at the walkie-talkie with disbelief, the final verse of 'Snoopy vs. the Red Baron' played, then was followed by the mellow, smooth-talking voice of a would-be disc jockey.

'And this is Mean, Musical Howling Mad Murdock, serving up platters and chatters, coming to you live from high atop Indian duuuuuuuuunes on a cool, cool night ...'

Meadows tossed aside the walkie-talkie with disgust and scurried back towards the rear of the truck, where Stark had already taken refuge. The two of them looked at each other nervously, shaking the sand from their guns.

'Let's nail the guys down here, then make a run for it,' Stark said. 'I'll take the guy outside, you get the driver.'

As the two SWAT officers were squirming on their bellies back towards the front of the truck, BA quickly picked up his walkie-talkie inside the van and passed along the information to Face and Murdock, who promptly took aim on the truck and sent another volley of rifle fire crashing down, just missing Stark and Meadows.

'Toss your guns out where we can see 'em,' Hannibal ordered.

After a moment's hesitation, Stark and Meadows complied. 'You guys are good, man,' Stark conceded. 'I'll give you that.'

'And you guys are finished,' Hannibal told them. 'Tomorrow morning the resignations and the confessions. If not, you die. And you die hard.'

With that, Hannibal got back into the car. BA doused the lights and wheeled the van about, then headed off into the night, leaving Stark and Meadows to contemplate the ultimatum and their near-executions.

TWELVE

The others might have felt fear in the wake of their humiliation at Indian Dunes, but Dolph Stark's reaction wavered between rage and frustration. Back home at his apartment, he spent most of the night pacing, hashing over the events of the past few days, trying to sort out clues as to the identities of his tormentors. At one point he was ready to drive all the way to Ed Maloney's house on his own and drag the officer out of bed for an explanation, but he figured that Maloney had probably moved himself and his family to a motel or else he'd be sleeping with a gun at his side, ready to fire at anyone who came on his property unannounced. Fatigue finally caught up with Stark at three in the morning, and he dozed off for a few hours of fitful sleep before the alarm jangled him back to reality a little past dawn.

As he was driving to work, Stark shifted his mental gears and tried focusing on the way his antagonists were operating. He was most concerned about their ability to overhear conversations between himself and the other SWAT officers, and he tried to recall all the incidents where he knew he and his men had been eavesdropped upon. Methodically narrowing down the means by which the buggings might have been achieved, he eliminated all but two possibilities. Either the enemy had access to a supersensory electronic ear that could somehow pick up sounds from afar, or else they had managed to plant bugs on the men themselves.

'Bugs! That's it!' he cried out triumphantly as he pulled into the parking lot next to SWAT headquarters. Bounding out of his car, he strode hastily into the building and confronted the desk sergeant.

'What say, Dolph?' the sergeant asked, noticing the look in Stark's eye.

'Those folks who were in the locker rooms spraying for cockroaches,' Stark said, 'Did they leave a billing address or phone number where they could be reached?'

'Why, no ...' the sergeant replied. 'Before they left they called in to their boss and he told them not to charge us for spraying. Something about doing their part in helping a good cause. Pretty weird, huh?'

'I knew it!' Stark said, thumping his fist on the desk. 'That's when they did it!'

'Did what, Captain?'

'Never mind,' Stark said, starting off down the hallway.

'They weren't legit, were they,' the sergeant called out after Stark.

Stark stopped and turned back to face the other officer. 'What makes you say that?'

'Well, when they showed up, they said Louie had called them about the cockroaches, but when Louie showed up and I talked to him, he said he didn't know anything about it.' The sergeant offered up a sheepish smile and added, 'Sorry I didn't look into it more at the time, Captain. Hope it didn't create too big a problem. What's happened anyway? Does this have anything to do with the SWAT truck getting shot up late last night?'

'Thanks for the info,' Stark said, ducking the question. He continued down the hall to the locker rooms and pushed his way inside. Meadows, Shaeffer, and Collins were all in front of their lockers, suiting up in their uniforms as they discussed the previous evening. Seeing Stark, they all fell silent and looked the other way.

'Let's meet up in my office, pronto,' Stark told them as he went to his locker and quickly twirled the combination on his lock. 'And no shoptalk on the way, got it?'

'Why?' Collins asked. 'What's up?'

'Just do what I say!' Stark ordered.

As the others filed out of the room, Stark opened his locker and meticulously searched it from top to bottom. Finding nothing out of order, he slowly changed into his uniform, inspecting the shoes and each bit of clothing. It was while he was buttoning up his shirt that he found what he was looking for.

'Of course!' he said, tugging hard at the doctored button until it pulled free of his shirt. He stared at it for a moment, then closed it in the meat of his palm as he left the room and bounded upstairs, where the others had already gathered outside the door to his office. He unlocked the door and let them in.

'So, Captain,' Shaeffer said, sitting down on the edge of Stark's desk. 'What's our next move? I'm all –'

Before Shaeffer could go on, Stark came over to him and grabbed at his collar. Shaeffer threw his hands up to defend himself, expecting that he was about to be hit, but Stark merely pulled hard at the button on his collar until it came free.

'Hey, what gives?' Shaeffer grumbled once Stark took his hands off him and moved over to Meadows.

Stark waited until he had the top buttons from Meadows' and Collins' uniforms, then threw them down on the desktop and said, 'That's how they were doing it! They had us every damned inch of the way!'

'With buttons, Captain?' Meadows said, still confused.

'We're wondering how the hell they're bugging every place we go before we get there ...' Stark paused and grabbed a hefty paperweight, slamming it down hard on the buttons. ' ... and we're carrying the mikes along with us!'

The others crowded around the desk and stared down at the crushed buttons, seeing the bits of transistorized circuitry that had been concealed inside them.

'I'll be damned,' Shaeffer muttered with disbelief as Stark swept the rubble from the desktop into a wastebasket. 'Those guys sure as hell are pros. CIA, do you think?'

'Whoever they are, they got us over a barrel,' Collins said, pulling a pack of cigarettes out of his pocket and lighting one up. His hands were shaking.

'Bull,' Stark said, pointing into the wastebasket. 'That's their barrel, Collins. We aren't over it any more.'

'I dunno, Captain,' Meadows said unsurely. 'Seems to me finding the mikes doesn't change our situation all that much.'

'The hell it doesn't!' Stark shot back, beginning to pace again.

'What about their threat?' Collins said, blowing smoke nervously out his nose. 'I mean, they said we had to turn ourselves in by today or else they were –'

'What!?' Stark took a long step towards Collins and swept up his arm, grabbing his cohort by the wrist and almost knocking the cigarette from Collins' hand. 'You think I'm gonna sign a piece of paper saying I'm a multiple murderer? You think any of you are?!!'

Stark let go of Collins and Collins rubbed his wrist where he'd been grabbed. 'They said they'd kill us,' Collins said, trying to blink away the smoke that was drifting up into his eyes. 'And it's not like they haven't been in a position to a few times already ...'

'Hey, where's your backbone, Collins!?' Stark warned. 'You're SWAT, the cream of the crop when it comes to nerves! Pull yourself together, damn it!' Turning on the others, he lectured, 'These guys aren't magicians, for crying out loud. They were only as good as their G-2. Now they're cut off. They can't second-guess us any more. Now I make my move!'

'What move is that?' Meadows asked him.

'Let me worry about that,' Stark told him. 'For now, you guys go on about your business. I'll join up with you later.'

Stark circled around behind his desk and eased into the padded contours of his swivel chair. He waited until the others had left the office and closed the door behind them, then picked up the phone and dialled a number. He got an answer on the fifth ring.

'Douglas Electronics. Can I help you?'

'Yeah, is this Alex?'

'Sure is.'

'Al, this is Dolph,' Stark said as he reached around the side of his desk and into the wastebasket, pulling out one of the battered buttons. 'I need to do a little eavesdropping, and I wondered if you could give give me a hand ...'

THIRTEEN

Grant Eldridge, managing editor of the Courier-Express, cupped his hand over the phone and shouted across the bustling newsroom, 'Hey, Allen!'

Amy was standing near the water cooler, gossiping with a few other reporters. She turned her head at the mention of her name and scanned the sea of desks, trying to spot her boss. He turned out to be leaning out of his office along the north wall.

'Yes, Mr Eldridge, what is it?'

'Long distance for you. Line three. From Bad Rock.'

'Bad Rock!' Amy gasped. 'Is it Commonble?'

'Yes, and he's calling collect, so hurry it up!'

Anticipation surged through Amy's veins as she started out of the room, calling to Eldridge over her shoulder, 'I'll take it in my office!'

'Tell that gumshoe he better start coming up with some decent leads or else he can start paying for his own calls,' Eldridge grumbled before retreating back inside his cubicle.

Amy hurried to her office and turned on the word processor perched upon her desk. Settling it behind the keyboard, she plucked up the phone and cradled it between her ear and her shoulder as she braced herself to type out the information Commonble had to tell her. He told her plenty. She typed relentlessly for the next twenty minutes, pausing only when she had a question or needed clarification of the many points Commonble was bringing up. He'd been right

82

about being on the verge of a major breakthrough. By the time Amy hung up, she was sure that her story was going to end up running page one for at least a week. She envisioned her name being put into nomination for a Pullitzer Prize, and as she started revising the notes, in the back of her mind she began plotting the scenario for her acceptance speech at next year's award banquet.

'Incredible,' she whispered to herself as she scanned the processor's display terminal and reread the highlights of her conversation with Commonble.

'What's incredible?' a voice called out from the doorway. Amy jerked in place, startled by the interruption. She glanced up to see Hannibal peering in through the half-opened door. 'I knocked twice,' he told her.

'Oh, I'm sorry, Hannibal,' Amy apologized. 'But you won't believe what I just found out from Commonble about what's happening up in Bad Rock!'

'That's good,' Hannibal said, 'Because you won't believe what we just found out about our boys in blue down here in LA. They found the mikes.'

'Oh, no. That's terrible.'

'I could think of other adjectives that come closer to the mark,' Hannibal said. 'At any rate, we've got to implement another plan now, and you're the ace up our sleeve.'

'Me?' Amy said. 'Poor, defenseless, womanly me?'

'Okay, Amy. Enough sarcasm. Now, can you help us or not?'

'You mean right now?'

'If you can swing it, yes.'

Amy sighed and filed her notes into the processor's memory before shutting it off. The Pulitzer Prize was going to have to be put on hold for the time being. Picking up the phone and dialling a number, she asked Hannibal, 'How long do you need me for?'

Hannibal checked his watch. 'Well, the SWAT shift gets off in half an hour. I'd say we'll need you an hour. Two max.'

Someone answered the phone and Amy told them, 'I'm going to take a long dinner break, then come back and put in a few more hours, okay? Pass the word to boss man for me, will you?'

'Good show,' Hannibal said as Amy grabbed her purse and headed for the doorway. 'I knew we could count on you.'

'Let me guess,' she said as she locked her office and the two of them headed for the elevators. 'You want to use me for bait.'

Hannibal let out a light laugh. 'Well, I guess that's one way of putting it. Not the way I'd put it, but –'

'Never mind, Hannibal,' Amy said. 'I'll be glad to help out. What I was going to tell you back in the office is that it turns out Stark and his men are connected with what's happening up in Bad Rock. I just found out.'

'Say what?'

The elevator doors opened and they stepped in, pushing for the basement. No one else was with them so Amy went on, 'It seems that Stark and Shaeffer co-own one of the trailers where the heaviest gambling goes down. They bought in a little over six months ago.'

Hannibal pictured a calendar in his mind and counted back six months, then said, 'That's about the time the killings started, according to Maloney.'

'No mere coincidence, I'll bet you,' Amy said. 'Anyway, that's just the tip of the iceberg. Stark has a kid brother who lives up that way by the name of Jenko, and he's part –'

'Jenko Stark?' Hannibal muttered. 'How'd his mother come up with a name like that?'

'When you name your first kid Adolph, anything's possible, I guess. Anyway, this Jenko heads up a biker gang, of all things, and Commonble says they've been responsible for providing the trailer whorehouse up there with most of the runaway girls that end up turning tricks. Some story, huh? There's more to it, of course, but those are the headlines.'

As the elevator slowed to a stop and opened its doors to the basement, Hannibal pulled a cigar from his pocket and fingered with the cellophane as they headed for the A-Team van, parked in its customary place around the corner. 'Things are starting to fall into place, Amy,' he said, conjecturing aloud. 'With Maloney's help, we checked into the victims of our SWAT friends, and more than half of them had a flair for gambling and a variety of other vices. It wouldn't surprise me if Stark and the others got their start bumping off folks who squelched on some debts.'

'And they were probably hired out by the same mobsters who run the whole operation up in Bad Rock,' Amy joined in the speculation. 'It all makes sense. Once they earned a reputation for their dirty work, they probably started taking referral business from people like Delgado's brother.'

'Well, I think it's time to put these people out of business,' Hannibal said, biting the tip of his cigar and spitting it out the side of his mouth. 'Once we clean up things around here, maybe we'll take a little trip up to Bad Rock and see what we can do ...'

'That might not be necessary,' Amy said. 'Commonble's got the ear of a district attorney up there. Once they put together a little more evidence, it looks like the feds are going to move in and close down the operation in one fell swoop.'

'Oh,' Hannibal looked disappointed. 'I was just starting to look forward to tangling with the mob.'

'It seems to me you'll have plenty of chances to get on the jazz down here,' Amy said.

'Maybe you're right.' As they reached the van, Amy began to open the side door to get in back. Hannibal stopped her, shaking his head. 'You're not coming with us, Amy.'

'What?' Amy cried out, exasperated. 'I thought I was going to be your trump card ...'

'You are,' Hannibal assured her, 'But the plan calls for you to do some solo driving.'

'Solo driving?' Amy frowned. 'You mean by myself?'

Up in the front seat of the van, Templeton Peck rolled down the window and grinned at Amy. That's what the man said. All by your lonesome. Your big chance ...'

Amy let out a deep breath and reached into her purse for her car keys, mumbling, 'I can hardly wait ...'

FOURTEEN

Stepping out of SWAT headquarters, Al Collins whistled to himself. It wasn't a carefree whistle, however. It was more like the whistle of a tea kettle venting excess pressure. Collins was still on edge, despite Stark's assurances all day long that things would be taken care of and they wouldn't have to worry about harassment much longer. Stark had even gone so far as to suggest that the four of them band together over the weekend and take a run up to Bad Rock, where they could squeeze in a couple days of nonstop partying and sampling the nubile pleasures to be had at Stark's and Meadow's trailer. With that in mind, Friday couldn't come soon enough for Collins.

'Hey, hey, maybe I won't have to wait that long after all,' he suddenly whispered to himself, pausing at the foot of the steps to feast his eyes on Amy, who was standing in the parking lot with a look of consternation as she peered under the hood of her car. She jiggled a few wires, then circled around and slipped in behind the wheel to try to start the engine. It turned over several times, but wouldn't catch. Frustrated, Amy jerked her key out of the ignition and slammed the door as she moved back around to the front of the car, catching a glimpse of Collins out of the corner of her eye.

'Well, well, a damsel in distress,' Collins sniggered to himself as he stuffed his hands into the pockets of his civvies and strolled over.

'Why now?' Amy was asking the car. 'Why couldn't you

wait until I was closer to home, darn you!'

When there was no reply under the hood, Collins joked, 'I guess your engine's pleading the fifth.'

Amy turned to Collins, wiping the bangs from her face with the back of her hand. 'Excuse me?'

'Pleading the fifth,' Collins repeated with a smile. '"I refuse to answer that question on the grounds that it may incriminate me." A little comic relief.'

'Oh.' Amy offered up a frail smile. 'I could use a lot more than a little relief, believe me. I parked in here because I didn't have change for a meter, and look what happens to me. I can't believe my luck!'

'Let me take a look and see if I can't help,' Collins offered, widening his smile.

'Oh that's okay,' Amy insisted with a wave of her head. 'It's just my electric ignition. It's been on the fritz all week, but I haven't gotten around to replacing it. If I just wait a few minutes, I'm sure it will start up. In the meantime, I think I could use a drink. You know any place a working girl can have a happy hour special or two?'

'Well, as a matter of fact, there's a great little place about a mile from here,' Collins suggested. 'I was just headed there myself. If you don't mind riding shotgun on a motorcycle, I'd be glad to give you a lift.'

Amy thought it over as she stared at her car, then slammed down the hood and said, 'Mister, you've got yourself a deal!'

'The name's Al,' Collins said, pointing over at the 750 Yamaha he'd driven to work instead of his Datsun. 'And there's my trusty steed.'

'Oh, this should be fun,' Amy said, following Collins over to the bike and deftly straddling the back part of the seat. 'I haven't done this in years. Oh, by the way, my name is Joan. Joan Hobbs.'

'A real pleasure to meet you, Miss Hobbs.'

'Joan. Call me Joan. Let's go have a quick party!'

Collins climbed onto the bike and started it up, shouting over the deep rumble of the engine, 'You're on!'

The mufflers on the Yamaha had been modified to cut down their effectiveness, and it was too loud for them to

87

carry on any semblance of a conversation. Amy waited until they reached the bar, then strung Collins along for two drinks, convincing him she was a sales representative for Hobbit House Toys, staying at the Holiday Inn down the road while she was in town on business. She also threw in enough bogus autobiographical tidbits for Collins to feel that he's stumbled upon the answer to every male swinger's dream. When, after polishing off her second Mai Tai, Amy suggested that Collins take her over to her hotel room for a few lines of some cocaine she'd brought along for just such an occasion, he was more than willing to oblige. With Collins mildly inebriated by liquor and lust, the ride to the motel ranked high on Amy's list of death-defying experiences, but she tried not to show any concern for fear of blowing her cover. She was feeling lightheaded herself, even though she'd spilled more than half of both her drinks onto the carpet back at the bar, and when Collins started putting the make on her the moment they entered the hotel stairwell leading to the second floor, it was all she could do to fend off his advances.

'Not here, doll,' she cooed, taking Collins by the hand and leading him up the steps. 'Don't be tacky. Let's wait til we get to my room, then we'll do things right, okay?'

'Sure thing, Joanie,' Collins drawled, struggling to keep up with Amy. 'I like the way you think, woman.'

'I'm glad you do,' Amy chuckled as they reached the hallway and headed for her room. She drew a hotel key from her purse and pretended to have trouble fitting it into the lock.

'Allow me,' Collins said, placing his hand over Amy's and guiding the key home.

'Thank you, kind sir,' Amy giggled, opening the door.

Collins was on her the moment she turned the nob, drawing her into his embrace like a squid in heat. They backpedalled into the room, and Amy was barely able to reach out with her foot to close the door behind them.

'Okay, baby, this is it,' Collins promised as he tried to plant his lips on Amy's. She turned her head to avoid his aim, at the same time glancing into the room and discovering, to her relief, that they weren't alone.

'You're damn right this is it,' Hannibal told Collins as Face snapped off a flash photograph of the would-be swingers.

Collins whirled away from Amy, almost colliding with Howling Mad Murdock, who drifted out of the kitchen area with an automatic pistol trained on the dumbfounded officer.

'You better know right now,' Collins sputtered, trying to muster up a trace of sobriety. 'I'm a cop.'

'I could debate that statement,' Hannibal said as he stepped forward and reached inside Collins jacket withdrawing the man's Magnum. Hannibal turned the gun on Collins, allowing Murdock a chance to take Amy's place next to the officer.

'Say cheese,' Murdock urged.

'Beautiful!' Face said, taking another picture.

'What is this?!' Collins demanded. 'I want to know...' His voice trailed off as he took a long look at Face.

'Recognize your rock climbing buddy from last night?' Hannibal asked him.

Collins' last vestige of courage withered away with the realization as to who he was dealing with. Holding his hands out to his sides in a gesture of willing surrender, he licked his lips and rambled, 'Oh, hey ... hey, look, we been talking all morning about how we should do that ... you know, sign the confession and all? I'd do it in a hot second ... I think Meadows might, too. It's Stark, y'know ... he's got the goods on us. He's the one.'

Hannibal was working on one of his ever-present cigars. Blowing smoke Collins' way, he grinned. 'I had a feeling there might be a little hesitation on your parts, so I decided we'd need one of you to fink.'

'Guess who drew the short straw,' BA boomed out, entering the gathering from the adjacent bedroom and sending a fresh shiver of fear down Collins' spine.

'What're ya talkin' about?' Collins said, his voice slurring.

'You're going to turn state's evidence on your friends, Casanova,' Amy informed him, relishing the moment.

'Stark would kill me if I tried anything!' Collins wailed.

Gesturing to his camera, Face said, 'Stark'll kill you anyway once I send him these photographs of you and us sitting here so nice and cozy, chatting about who you guys did and didn't kill.'

While Collins let Face's words sink in, Hannibal moved in and draped an arm across his shoulder, offering an endearing smile for the next picture. Sobered by the confrontation, Collins finally decided to try to tough it out. He told Hannibal, 'It'd just be one cop's word against another's. There's no evidence to convict any of us.'

Hannibal moved aside and motioned for BA to take his turn having a group portrait taken with Collins. 'How about the murder weapons?' Hannibal asked. 'Ballistics tests go over great in a court of law.'

'We're not ding-dongs,' Collins answered hotly. 'The weapons are clean when we get 'em. We get the weapons from the evidence room. We put 'em back when we're done. Since they've been impounded and tagged before we borrow 'em, nobody'd think of tying them into our jobs.'

'Then they're still in the impound room,' Hannibal surmised, 'and you can go get them.'

'Well, it's not all that easy ...'

'Get 'em!' BA shouted at Collins before cracking a grin long enough for Face to take their picture.

'Yeah, yeah,' Collins blurted, eyeing BA's biceps. 'Sure, I can get them, but ... I could wind up in the gas chamber!'

Face was using a polaroid camera, which spat out its pictures moments after they were taken. Hannibal took the shots that had already been taken and waved them in front of Collins' face, telling him, 'If I send these photos on over to Stark, they'll be tossing dirt on your box by the end of the week.'

'That leaves me bumping off walls no matter which way I spin,' Collins complained.

'If you turn state's evidence, that could buy you a reduced sentence,' Face advised him. 'From where I'm standing, that should be looking a might cushy right now.'

'Get those guns,' Hannibal said. 'You'll turn them over to

Inspector Maloney, along with your signed confession explaining what you and your three buckaroos have been doing.'

'Yeah ... yeah.' Collins bobbed his head like an overeager puppy. 'Yeah, I'll get them and meet you ...'

A mile way, Dolph Stark and Adam Meadows were listening in on the conversation through a monitor speaker propped up on Stark's desk.

'Good,' Hannibal was saying, 'We'll have Maloney at the Oceanside Amusement Park at sundown. Be there with the goods and you might save your neck.'

Stark leaned over and snapped off the speaker. 'Collins, you wimp, this is one time I was counting on you to belly up.'

'Nice move, Captain, beating them at their own game by planting a bug on Collins,' Meadows told Stark. 'I love it.'

'Never let it be said I don't learn by example,' Stark said with a grin. He checked his watch. 'I figure we got about two hours. Let's get ahold of Shaeffer and suit up. It's been a long time since I've been to the park ...'

Meadows let out a low, menacing laugh as they headed for the door. 'Those guys'll never know what hit 'em ...'

FIFTEEN

Oceanside Amusement Park was between owners and closed to the public. Seagulls and terns had free reign of the facilities, and they glided gracefully above the elevated rides, carried on strong currents of coastal breeze. The smell of brine was in the air and the temperature was just beginning to dip as the sun closed in on the distant horizon of deep blue sea. The entrances to the park were boarded up, but there were several points along the rambling perimeter where it was possible for someone to squeeze through the space between missing planks or hop a short length of fence. Al Collins had no problems getting in, even when he was toting a hefty black satchel filled with the evidence Hannibal had demanded from him earlier. As a precaution against the possibility that he might run into a security guard, Collins was wearing his SWAT uniform and toting a gun on his hip. As far as the uninitiated were concerned, Collins was at the park on assignment, acting on a tip that someone had left the satchel at the park for authorities to pick up to aid in their investigation of a number of recent murders.

Because the facilities were up for sale, they were well-maintained, and Collins strode down the spotless walkways, flanked by buildings bright with fresh coats of paint. In addition to the usual assortment of thrill rides, there were several theme areas designed and decorated in motifs ranging from Old West to Gay Nineties to Roaring Twenties. Costumed mannequins were posted outside of gift shops, sporting period fashions for sale inside. Collins almost pulled his gun on a dummy dressed up as a racketeer before he ralized it wasn't real. He was back to his high-strung, apprehensive self, and every time the wind creaked through one of the rides, he'd spin around, ducking behind the nearest cover, fearing that he'd be gunned down by Hannibal's men and left to die while they walked off with the satchel.

As Collins walked past the roller coaster, a figure crouched behind the cover of the ticket booth, peering around the corner. It was Meadows, and he stayed put until Collins was out of earshot, then slowly raised a walkie-talkie to his lips, whispering, 'He just passed the coaster, heading for the arcade.'

'I see him,' Stark's voice crackled over the speaker. 'Circle around. Shaeffer and I will stay on him.'

Meadows slipped out of the shadows, carrying an automatic rifle. Crossing the walkway, he cut through a group of still figures poised in front of a Western theme shop, almost knocking over a wooden Indian holding a cigar box. Once he had turned the corner and vanished from sight, one of the figures moved. Hannibal, dressed in the black garb of a gunslinger, stepped down from the porch, pausing long enough to help himself to one of the Indian's cigars before heading off to trail Meadows. He propped the cigar between his lips but didn't light it.

Stark was posted behind the grove of trees shading a concession area, and across from him Shaeffer was hunched behind a cart on the entrance ramp to the funhouse, framed from behind by the painted face of a laughing clown. As they watched on, each armed with their own automatic rifles, Collins passed down the midway between them, taking purposeful strides until he reached the string of boarded-up arcades that housed games of chance when the park was open. He stopped there and looked around. Both Stark and Shaeffer slipped out of view. Moments later, someone called out, 'Collins.'

Collins whirled around just as Peck stepped through the curtains of a fortune-teller's booth.

'That the stuff?' Peck asked, pointing at the satchel.

'What do you think it is, my lunch?' Collins said testily.

'Funny man,' Face said, reaching out for the satchel.

'Where's Maloney?' Collins said.

'Let us worry about that, pal.' Face opened the satchel and peered inside. Satisfied with what he saw, he put his fingers to his lips and let out a shrill whistle. Murdock and BA emerged from behind two of the nearby arcade booths and came over to join Collins and Face. Murdock frisked Collins and took his gun.

'So what happens to me now?' Collins asked. 'Look, if you were to let me walk outta here, I'd be out of the state by midnight. I can cop a new identity and start clean. With the confession and the murder weapons there, you'll be able to nail the other guys without my –'

'Shut up, fool!' BA told Collins.

'Here's the deal,' Face explained. 'Maloney's waiting for us over at the last booth. You wait here while we go have him take a look at this stuff you've brought. If he thinks he has enough for convictions, we'll take you in and let you plea bargain your way to a lighter sentence. Fair enough?'

Collins heaved a sigh of resignation, nodding bleakly.

As Face, Murdock and BA headed off for the booth, Face glanced over his shoulder and told the offcier, 'Oh, by the way, if you're thinking of trying to make a run for it while we're gone, remember you aren't alone out here. Our boss is keeping an eye on you. One false move and he uses you for target practise. And he doesn't miss.'

Collins watched the three members of the A-Team go over to the last of the boarded-up arcades and slip inside through a side door. He reached to his shirt pocket for his cigarettes, and as he lit one up, he started looking around the park to see if he could spot Hannibal. The sky overhead was growing dark, and the long shadows cast by the setting sun seemed to have a life of their own. He surveyed the roller coaster, the Ferris wheel, the spinning saucers ride, the rooftops of the theme shops, but he could see no trace of Hannibal. As he turned around to check in the other direction, though, he suddenly froze in terror and the cigaretes tumbled from his lips.

Meadows was standing three feet away from him, the barrel of his rifle pointed at his face.

'One word and you're dead,' Meadows whispered lethally, keeping his weapon trained on Collins as both Stark and Shaeffer emerged from their hiding places and quietly rushed over. Collins blanched with terror at finding himself surrounded by the three men he was trying to condemn in hopes of saving his life. From the looks on their faces, he could guess that they knew he'd betrayed them.

'Listen, guys, let me explain,' Collins stammered. 'I was settin' them up, that's all. I figured I'd lead –'

Stark swung around behind Collins and whipped up the butt of his rifle, catching his fellow officer in the back of the head. Knocked unconscious, Collins fell limply into the dirt at the other men's feet.

'You'll get what's coming to you once we finish the others,' Stark promised. Signalling for Shaeffer and Meadows to spread out, the three gunmen converged upon the arcade the A-Team had entered moments before, taking up positions whereby they could unload a cross-fire into the clapboard structure from as many directions as possible without shooting into one another. Once in place, each of the men slowly raised their rifles and drew aim on one side of the booth.

'What's a carnival without a shooting range?' Stark said under his breath as he gave the signal to fire. The lingering silence gave way to the hammering fury of three automatics pumping full clips of ammunition into the flimsy arcade booth. The structure quaked from the force of the shelling and all four walls were pocked with bulletholes. Because all three men had earned ribbons for their rifle-handling, none of the shots missed their mark, and there was no portion of the walls, from top to bottom, that had been spared from the riddling assault.

When they were out of ammunition, the officers lowered their rifles and paused to admire the destruction they'd wreaked on the building, then moved forward in unison, meeting outside the doorway. They were confident that no one could have survived the ambush, but still they exercised caution. Stark and Shaeffer stood flush against the walls on either side of the doorway while Meadows took a deep breath, then kicked the door in and ducked to one side.

Nothing happened.

Stark was the first one to go in, followed closely by Meadows and Shaeffer. They let out a simultaneous chorus of disbelieving cries at the sight awaiting them. The ground dirt of the arcade floor was scarred with bulletholes and littered with bits of splintered wood, but there were no bodies. Face, BA, and Murdock were nowhere to be seen.

'What the hell?' Stark said, dumbfounded.

'Where did they go?' Meadows wondered aloud.

Just then there was a scraping sound overhead. Before the officers could react, the three members of the A-Team dropped down from the rafters like over-ripe fruit, landing amidst their foes with a flurry of fists. Stark and Shaeffer quickly lost their guns and were staggering off the walls from the force of the blows dealt by BA and Peck. Meadows had managed to elude the brunt of Murdock's assault and he bolted for the door in hopes of escaping, only to find himself staring at twin six-shooters in the hands of Hannibal, who stood in the doorway like Marshall Dillon about to foil a bank robbery in Dodge City.

'By all means, come on out,' Hannibal told Meadows. 'Only put your hands on your head. I hear a rumour the sky's falling. You, too, Stark and Shaeffer. Nice and easy. Any tricks will be your last.'

Hannibal backed away from the doorway, letting the three SWAT officers file out into the dusk air as Murdock reached up and pulled down the black satchel from the rafters.

'You guys okay?' Hannibal asked his partners.

Dusting himself off, Face told him, 'We're fine. Amazing, isn't it, how expert marksmen will never shoot above the chest level of their intended target?'

'Absolutely,' Hannibal said.

On his way out the door, Murdock paused long enough to pull a safety match from his pocket. He snapped the tip against his thumbnail, then used the match to light Hannibal's cigar, babbling, 'I'm telling you, Hannibal, you should have seen the way we scrambled up onto those rafters. Regular circus types, we were. Agile, we swung through the air with –'

'– with the greatest of ease. Yeah, I get the picture, Murdock.'

Ed Maloney was outside, too, standing guard over Collins, who was beginning to come to. Hannibal took the satchel from Murdock and skimmed it across the ground to Maloney. 'Here you go, Inspector. The whole shebang. Confession and all. Of course, we've got these clowns dead to rights for attempted murder tonight –'

Maloney took his eyes of Collins and crouched over to pick up the satchel. It proved to be a crucial mistake, as Collins was more alert than he'd let on. Lunging forward, he bowled Maloney over, knocking the man's gun to the ground. Collins picked it up on the run and fired a few wild shots back at the men gathered around the arcade booth to cover his escape. The distraction was sufficient to give the other SWAT officers a last, desperate chance at freedom, too. Meadows grabbed Murdock by the wrist and jerked him off-balance so that he staggered headlong into Hannibal. Face and BA had dived to the ground to avoid getting hit by Collins' gunfire, and by the time they were back on their feet, Shaeffer and Stark were rushing off in separate directions. Meadows was already out of sight.

The chase was on.

Thinking fast, Ed Maloney swung the satchel in a wide arc around his head, then let fly with it at the retreating figure of Collins. His aim was good, and the satchel slammed into the back of Collin's legs as he was in mid-stride. Not suspecting the blow, Collins spun to one side, tripping over the kerb and crashing into a cluster of knee-high trash cans. Before he could get back up on his feet, Templeton Peck came flying through the air and landed on top of him, subduing him long enough for Maloney to join them and regain possession of his gun.

Murdock's pursuit of Meadows coursed past the concession stand and towards the teacup ride. Seeing that Meadows was running around the edge of the ride, Murdock threw caution to the wind and lept over the railing onto the raised platform. Dodging the inert, oversized cups, he crossed the diameter of the ride, reaching the other side just as Meadows was running past him.

'It's the daring young man on the flying trapeeeeeze!' Murdock sang out, launching himself on a brief, self-propelled flight that ended with him docking himself on Meadows' back and tackling the officer to the ground. Before Meadows could put up any resistance, his downward momentum was interrupted by the railing of the teacup ride and he was knocked unconscious. As he was rolling clear of his victim, Murdock noticed a plastic-coated card that had dropped from Meadows' shirt onto the walkway. Picking it up, he read aloud, 'You have the right to remain silent. Anything you say can and will be used against you in a court of law . . .'

As he continued reading Meadows his rights, Murdock heard a car engine starting up. Straining his neck, he glanced over the top of a nearby shrub and saw Shaeffer trying to make his getaway in the same crumpled grey sedan the SWAT officers had used during their attempted assasination of Delgado earlier in the week. Shaeffer was picking up speed and heading for the service entrance through which he, Stark and Meadows had entered the park. It didn't seem that he was going to be stopped until a hulking figure suddenly burst into view, rushing sideways towards the vehicle.

'Fly, BA, fly!' Murdock shouted.

Whether or not he heard Murdock, BA did spring forward and dive headlong through the air, landing with brutal force on the hood of the sedan. Behind the wheel, Shaeffer let up on the gas and squirmed in his seat, trying to see around BA, who was blocking his view through the windshield.

'Stop this car, fool!' BA roared. When Shaeffer jerked hard on the steering wheel, trying to shake him off the hood, BA responded by ramming his fist through the windshield and grabbing the wheel himself. Stunned by BA's action, Shaeffer lost control of the vehicle and, in his panic, he pressed the accelerator to the floor. The car screech violently to the right and barrelled forward. BA barely was able to pull his arm out of the windshield and roll clear of the hood before the runaway sedan bounded over a kerb and hit a pitched embankment at such an angle that the car flipped sideways as it vaulted through the air a dozen yards or more. Landing on its good side, the sedan came to a quick halt. BA rose to his feet, ignoring a few minor bruises, and rushed towards the totalled vehicle. Shaeffer wriggled out of the side window, a disoriented look on his face. He wasn't about to put up any resistance when BA came over to apprehend him.

That left Stark, who had thus far, eluded Hannibal and taken refuge in the building that housed the motor for the sky ride that ran the length of the entire park. Still armed with his six-shooters, Hannibal warily approached the open-air structure, keeping his eyes and ears open for Stark.

'You've still got a crack at life in the slammer,' Hannibal called out. 'Beats dying on the spot if you force my hand.'

There was no answer inside the building.

Hannibal changed his course and silently circled around to the back entrance, which necessitated climbing a set of concrete steps. He had cleared the last of the steps and was poking his head inside the motor room when Stark suddenly jumped down from a crawlspace overhead. Hannibal was taken by surprise, and when Stark shoved him towards the railing next to one of the ride-cabs, he had to drop both his guns to prevent himself from stumbling over the rail and down the twenty foot dropoff.

'Always copying our moves, eh, Stark?' Hannibal cracked as he spun around to meet the officer's charge. Stark had managed to grab a foot-long wrench, and he brandished it like a club, just missing Hannibal's face by inches with a fierce swing. Hannibal grabbed Stark's wrist and the two men grappled feverishly across the room, each trying to get the upper hand on the other. They were too caught up in the struggle to waste time on words, and they punctuated their writhings with grunts and groans. At one point, Hannibal succeeded in slamming Stark hard against the wall behind him, but the blow didn't phase Stark, although he felt a jab of pain from where his shoulder had inadvertently struck the starting switch that activated the ride's motor.

As a slow procession of ride-cars began arriving and departing from the platform, Hannibal and Stark continued to be locked in close combat, clinging to one another to keep their fists from entering into the fray, Stark lost his grip on the wrench at one point, but other than that he showed no signs of yielding any advantage to Hannibal.

Inevitably, the two men wandered into the path of one of the ride-cars, which dangled from an overhead cable. Hannibal tried to slam Stark's head against the roof of the car, but the officer pulled away to avoid contact, at the same time swinging around so that Hannibal was between him and the lift. Somehow Hannibal's belt became caught in the framework of the car, and he found himself being lifted up into the air. Stark tried to pry himself free, but Hannibal held onto him tightly, and within seconds they were both off the ground, dangling from the lift as they headed out into the open. Each man freed one hand to secure a better grip on the cart, for they were rising quickly to an altitude in excess of thirty feet.

Hannibal almost fell when his belt broke free of whatever it had become caught upon, but at the last second he was able to light his second hand on an exposed rung sticking out of the front of the car. Once he had a firmer grip, he started deliberately swaying in such a way that he was able to start kicking Stark. Stark retaliated in kind, but his hold on the lift was more precarious, and when Hannibal locked their legs together and tugged with all his might, he was able to jerk the officer hard enough to break his grip. Stark's eyes went wide with shock as he fell away from the cart and dropped helplessly towards the ground. The slanted roof of a vendor's stand helped to break his fall somewhat, but he landed with a force that knocked him out and undoubtedly left him with countless broken bones.

Hannibal carefully pulled himself up into the car and plopped into one of the seats, drawing in a series of deep, quick breaths. He'd stared death in the face numerous times throughout his life, but it wasn't something he'd ever get used to.

For now, though, he could rest content ...

SIXTEEN

Ed Maloney was in high spirits when he dropped in at Hannibal's Bar for a pint of ale on his way home from work. It was league night for local dart enthusiasts, so the bar was alive with activity and enthusiasm, which suited Maloney fine. Aside from his cold, he was feeling the best he had in years. Giving Mick a dollar tip on a pint of cold ale, he took his drink over to one of the few vacant tables and settled down to read over the newspaper accounts of the arrests that had been handed down against Stark and the other SWAT officers accused of a spate of crimes ranging from conspiracy to murder. Amy had filed the story for the evening edition of the Courier-Express, and she'd skilfully given equal credit for the apprehension of Stark's men to both Maloney and the A-Team, although by the time authorities had arrived at the park to assist Maloney in bringing the assassins into custody, Hannibal and the others had already left the scene. Maloney smiled to himself as he read, knowing as he did the bulk of the story that lay between the lines. As he was turning the page, he suddenly let out a sneeze.

'Gesundheit,' a voice called out to him.

Maloney looked up to see Hannibal standing before him, smoking his cigar. 'How's the cold, Inspector? You feeling any better?'

'Hannibal!' Maloney cried out, surprised. 'Feelin' better? Are you kiddin'? I'm like a million bucks about now.' Pointing to the front page headlines, he added, 'I'm a hero downtown.'

'Even though you busted your fellow cops?' Hannibal asked. Behind him, Maloney could see the other members of the A-Team filing into the bar and making their way leisurely through the crowd to his table.

'The PD is made up of the best,' Maloney said, nodding greetings to the others. 'They'd don't like wires burning in their own house. Cancers like this are few and that's how we like it ... But I want to thank you ... all of you, including Miss Allen, for putting my name in the paper there. I don't deserve that much credit, though. You caught those guys, not me.'

As the A-Team was settling into seats around the table, Amy insisted, 'That's not true, Inspector. If you didn't have the strength to ignore their threats ... to go around a system you respect ... Stark and his cronies wouldn't have been caught. We all know that.'

'Which brings us to this ...' Hannibal reached into his pocket and pulled out a thick stack of bills and a bank book, tossing both onto the table in front of Maloney.

'What's that?' Maloney forwned. 'Hey, that cash is yours, fair and square. We had a deal.'

'Face, give him the score,' Hannibal said.

Peck withdrew a small notebook from his shirt pocket and started reading, 'Four mini bikes and monitoring equipment: fifteen hundred dollars; hot lights for the van: two hundred dollars; make-over job for the panel truck and assorted props for the exterminator scheme: four hundred. Floral display: seventy-five dollars. We already had our own walkie-talkies and some of the other things. And we're billing this one out at three-hundred a day per man ... and woman ... which is way below the going rate, but that's the way Hannibal wants it on this one. We're throwing in personal makeup, film, incidentals. Rounding everything out, we came up with ...' Face juggled the figures, moving his lips as he added them all up, arriving at a total. 'Thirty-six hundred and eighty dollars.'

'We already deducted it, Inspector,' Hannibal said. 'You keep the rest of your savings, put it to good use with that family of yours.'

Maloney stared at the money and bank book, then picked them both up and pocketed them, declaring, 'I think I got myself a real bargain. Thanks, it means a lot.'

'Hey, all things' considered, it was a lively few days,' Hannibal philosophized. 'The way we like 'em. Matter of fact, we're just on our way to do a bit of an encore.'

'How's that?' Maloney asked.

'Well it's a rather long, complicated story,' Hannibal said as he got up from his chair. 'We don't have time to go into it, but Amy's staying behind. She can fill you in if you're interested. For now, though, it's been a pleasure, Inspector ...'

Hannibal extended his hand. Maloney shook it, protesting, 'Where are you going? Can't you at least stay long enough for me to buy you a drink. Come on ...'

Face, BA, and Murdock all took turns shaking Maloney's hand as Hannibal explained, 'No can do. We have a long drive ahead of us, and if we dally we're apt to miss all the fireworks.'

Maloney rose from his seat, nearly tongue-tied with gratitude. 'Hey ... I don't know what else to ... I mean, I can't really find the right words to '

'Book, 'em, Dano,' Murdock suggested, doing an impression of his favourite Hawaiian law enforcer as he gave Maloney a pat on the back. 'Murder One.'

Perplexed, Maloney stayed where he was, watching the four men retrace their steps out of the bar, then he looked over at Amy, who was still seated at his table. 'That Murdock fellow, isn't he a little, well ... you know ... '

'Peculiar?'

'Yeah, that's one way of putting it.'

'You get used to it,' Amy assured him.

'Tell me, Amy,' Maloney said, waving at Mick to order up a round of drinks as he sat down. 'What's this encore they were talking about?'

Amy quickly related the background information about all the shady doings at the trailer park in Bad Rock, including Stark's and Meadow's ownership of one of the trailers used for prostitution and the reliance on Jenko Stark's bike gang to provide teenage girls for use at the facilities.

'Jenko, yeah, I remember hearing about him a few years back,' Maloney reflected. 'He used to run around down in these parts, gettin' into trouble all the time and making his brother go through a lot of flak at the station because of it. Been awhile since I've heard about him, though.'

'Well, at any rate,' Amy went on, 'my friend the private eye had it all worked out to where he was going to team up with the local D.A. and arrange for a massive raid on the trailer park tomorrow. Only now the D.A.'s come up with cold feet, Commonble says. I just talked to him a few hours ago, and he says the authorities want to hold off until they have more evidence, or so they say. He's afraid that the people at the trailer park are going to catch wind that they're in line for a bust and slip away before anything goes down. Right now, while we're sitting here, he's making a last-ditch appeal to the D.A. to follow through on their original plan. If the D.A. won't budge, Commonble's going to try making a move on his own. He's just one man against who knows how many others, though. When Hannibal heard about that, he decided it was time for the A-Team to get out of town for a few days. They should be in Bad Rock a little before dawn, ready for anything . . .'

Mick brought over two beers. Maloney hoisted his and proposed a toast, 'Well, I wish them the best of luck, whatever happens. To the A-Team!'

'I'll drink to that,' Amy said, chinking glasses with Maloney and putting down a sip of the cold ale.

'One thing I can't figure out, though,' Maloney confessed. 'Why do they do it? There's not all that much money in what they do.'

Amy smiled slyly and said. 'For the jazz, man. They do it for the jazz . . .'

SEVENTEEN

Before leaving Los Angeles, BA drove by the Veteran's Administration Hospital, dropping Howling Mad Murdock off along with a forged medical form stating that he'd undergone extensive testing and been found to be suffering from only a mild bronchial infection rather than the case of tuberculosis that had precipitated his release into Peck's care earlier in the week. Murdock had wanted to accompany the rest of the A-Team on their jaunt up to Bad Rock, but Hannibal had insisted that he check back into the hospital before the officials there got around to investigating his absence and discovering that he'd left under false pretenses. After making a second stop to fill up the van's gas tank, BA, Face, and Hannibal were finally on their way, driving nonstop through the night and alternating stints behind the wheel so that everyone could have a chance to squeeze in a couple hours of sleep.

Seven hours later, greyness bled into the black of night, then gave way to the warm bloom of the dawn sun. Traffic was light on the interstate, as it had been most of the night. The van whisked along the paved strip that cut through miles of undeveloped countryside, keeping pace with truckers en route to the next stop on their rambling itineraries. It was a no-man's land, where car radios could pick up stations from as far away as Arizona and Utah but nothing broadcast within a fifty mile radius. Power lines and sporadic billboards were the only signs of civilization aside from the freeway itself. Everything else was rolling hillside, scattered shrubs and an occasional majestic oak, all growing brighter by the moment in the morning light.

'Hard to believe there's Mafia-types around these parts,' BA mused, taking in the scenery.

'We're almost to Bad Rock,' Hannibal said, glancing up from a map. He was sitting next to BA in the front of the van while Face was sprawled out in back. 'Nevada's just over that ridgeline to the east. Don't let appearances fool you. If somebody could think of a quick way to make a crooked buck in the Arctic Circle, the mob would be there, ready to take over.'

'You're probably right, Hannibal,' BA admitted.

Face let out a rowdy yawn as he sat up in back and blinked his eyes, waking up. 'Mornin', campers! We almost there yet?'

'Another ten miles,' Hannibal informed him.

'Well, I don't know about you guys, but I could use a bite of breakfast,' Face said. 'I'd hate to be grappling with crazed bikers on an empty stomach.'

'It wouldn't break my heart if we didn't have to grapple with anyone,' Hannibal said, staring out the window. 'All this peace and quiet's putting me in the mood for a vacation. Maybe the feds will have moved in and cleaned things up without our help and we could knock off for a few days ... do some fishing and whatnot.'

BA laughed, 'It's not your style, man. You go on vacation and you'd end up bein' crazier than Murdock.'

'Maybe, BA, maybe. I'd sure like a chance to find out, though.'

Face rose to his knees and moved up near the others. Pointing through the windshield, he said, 'Well, here's a chance for a quickie vacation. Come on, BA, let's pull into this truck stop and grab some chow.'

'I need gas anyway,' BA said, slowing down and pulling off the freeway into the vast parking lot of a small diner surrounded by more than a dozen eighteen wheelers. There were a couple service islands off to one side, and BA pulled up alongside one of the pumps. As BA was getting out to fill the tank. Hannibal told Face, 'Why don't you go get something we can take along with us? This close to Bad Rock I don't want to lose any more time than we have to. As a matter of fact, I think I'll give Commonble a call from here and see if there's anything new to report.'

Hannibal walked over to the diner, alongside Peck, then broke away to use the outside phone booth. Feeding coins into the phone, he checked a scrap of paper in his shirt pocket for the private investigator's number and then dialled it. He counted off ten rings and was about to hang up when Commonble answered, sounding out of breath.

'Commonble here. Amy, is that you?'

'No, it's Hannibal Smith, Simon. We're almost there and I thought I'd just check in.'

'Oh, man, you missed it!' Commonble told him excitedly. 'The D.A. came through, after all. They raided the trailer park about an hour ago. I just got back! I'm tellin' ya, it was incredible! Caught most of the bastards with their pants down. Fired a few shots, but nobody got hurt ...'

'You're kidding!' Hannibal said. 'So it's all been done?'

'Well, practically. Jenko was there with his gang of bikers, and they were camped out in a field next to the park. We nabbed Jenko, but the others high-tailed it out of there while the cops were storming the trailers ... hey, where are you guys, anyway?'

Hannibal stuck his head out of the booth to check the sign over the diner. 'Hegiger's Truck Stop, just outside '

'Hegiger's!' Commonble shouted over the phone. 'Man, you're about a hundred yards from the road Jenko's gang'll be screamin' down tryin' to outrun the cops! If you know what's good for you, you'll stay put till they cruise by. There's about fifteen of them, and they are mean mothers, I'm tellin' ya!'

'I see ...' A strange gleam came to Hannibal's eyes as he stared through the glass door of the phone booth and saw the row of telephone poles marking the side road Commonble was talking about. 'Well, thanks for the warning, Simon. I'm glad I didn't wake you ...'

'Why don't you guys stop by at my place in Bad Rock?'

Commonble suggested. 'I'm at the Travel Lodge. I can give you some more material to bring back to Amy.'

'Yea, we might do that. Look, Simon, I gotta go.'

'Okay, man. Thanks for coming up. I hope you don't mind having missed out on the bust, but I couldn't get the cops to wait until you showed up.'

'That's all right, Simon. We'll talk to you later. Bye.' Hannibal hung up, then stuffed Commonble's number back into his pocket and pulled out a cigar in its place. He stepped out of the booth just as Face was leaving the diner, munching on a cinnamon swirl and carrying a take-out bag filled with doughnuts.

'Any news?'

'Cme on,' Hannibal said, picking up his stride as he headed for the van. 'We're back in business ...'

'What about our vacation?' Peck wondered, trying to keep up.'

'Like BA says, its' not my style ...'

EIGHTEEN

The side road was only two lanes wide, connecting Bad Rock with the interstate by bissecting a large parcel of farmland. A new corn crop was sprouting up from the soil, standing only shin high but promising to lunge upward in the coming months and produce enough tender ears to keep the land's owner from having to sell off more acreage to pay his property taxes. Barbed wire fencing surrounded the fields, erected so close to the shoulder of the road that anyone puling off to change a flat tyre would have to be a contortionist to get out of their car without impaling themselves on one of the taut, spiked knobs.

'Hey, Hannibal,' BA complained, 'No way we're stoppin' here to hassle wth them bikers. We get out here and somebody's gonna end up lookin' like shishakabob.'

'I couldn't agree more, BA,' Hannibal said, scanning the scenery as he tried to summon up an impromptu strategy. 'Keep going until we cross this bridge up here. If we don't see anything after that, then we'll just have to –'

'Hannibal, wait!' Face interrupted, holding a hand up for silence.

BA slowed down and all three men listened intently, finally hearing the drone of approaching engines. Looking down the road, a telltale cloud of rising dust further betrayed the advance of the bikers.

'Well, that sure doesn't leave us much time,' Hannibal observed wryly.

'What do we do, Hannibal?' BA asked, revving the engine but keeping his left foot on the clutch so that the van stayed put.

Hannibal weighed the situation a few moments, then said, 'I think we'll play a little game of chicken on the bridge . . .'

'Chicken? With a bunch of bikers?' BA made a face. 'It'll never work, man.'

'You got a better idea, I'm all ears,' Hannibal replied, opening the glove compartment and taking out his Browning automatic. When BA made it clear he had no alternatives, Hannibal looked back at Face, who was putting away the last of his second cinammon swirl. 'Get the Thompson ready. I got a feeling we're gonna need it.'

'Fine.' Face cracked, 'but if I get indigestion from having to rush my breakfast, you're going to hear about it.'

'Look, Face, if we pull this off, we'll go into Bad Rock and I'll buy you a *real* breakfast.'

'Okay, you're on!' Face grabbed the submachine gun and quickly inspected it to make sure it was ready for use. Hannibal released the safety on his pistol. BA kept the engine racing without letting up on the clutch and stared straight ahead, awaiting the first sight of the bike gang.

He didn't have to wait long. Within moments they were speeding into view. Simon Commonble had guessed right. There were fifteen of them, riding three abreast and five deep, hogging both lanes of the road. Wearing the regalia of alienation - stained denim, chains, and leather - they looked like disgruntled misfits who'd just missed passing their initiation into the Hell's Angels and were on the lookout for somebody to take it out on. Each of them was an unwashed bundle of bad news straddling a customized Harley that roared down the road with its mufflers giving off a sound like flatulence ushered forth from the very bowels of hell. In the absence of Jenko Stark, the leadership reins were in the hands of a man called Snake, who rode at the head of the formation, a soiled red bandana knotted around his head in the manner of a buccaneer. He was wearing the gang's colours on the back of his denim vest, and there were enough death's head images cluttering his clothes, bike, and body to make him a one-man celebration of All Soul's Day.

As they approached the bridge, which was only one lane wide and spanning a trickling stream, the bikers drew in closer without easing off on their throttles. At the same time, BA slowly began letting up on his clutch, muttering to Hannibal, 'I don't gotta wait until I see the whites of their eyes, do I?'

'Naw,' Hannibal said. 'Just gun it halfway across the bridge, then pull a brodie and we'll have ourselves an instant blockade. Then all we have to do is keep them busy until the cops catch up.'

'You sure make it sound easy, Hannibal,' BA snarled. Glancing into his rear-view mirror, he said, 'You better keep me covered, Face.'

'I've never let you down before, have I, BA?'

'You want me to count the times, sucker?'

'BA ...' Hannibal said, staring at the way before him. 'I think I see your cue.'

The bikers were now less then fifty yards from the bridge, the same distance away as the A-Team. Popping the clutch, BA brought the van lurching fiercely forward, leaving a thin skin of rubber on the roadway. Entering the bridge simultaneously, the two forces raced headlong on their collision. Snake was the first to go to his brakes, followed immediately by the men on either side of him. Their bikes began to skid sideways, giving off shrill squeals as tyres bit for traction. Soon all fifteen bikes were braking, but reaction times were as varied as the grabbing power of each cycle's brakes, and there was a profusion of swearing as choppers slid into one another and their riders had their legs pinned between their own frames and those of others. At the same time, the A-Team van went into its skid, coming to a stop less then a dozen yards from the bikers and covering the width of the lane so completely that no one could have walked, much less driven past them. The passenger's side of the van was facing the bikers, and Hannibal rolled down his window, drawing aim on Snake with his Browning.

'Going somewhere, boys?'

Snake crawled free of his bike and stared at Hannibal. He

was reaching to his waist for a revolver but stopped when Hannibal fired a shot that missed taking off one of Snake's toes by mere inches.

'Nobody else try anything either,' Hannibal warned. 'My partner's got a submachine gun, and he'd just love to give you boys a few extra navels.'

In the back of the van, Fame slammed the butt of his palm against the stock of the Thompson, then whispered with exasperation, 'Damn thing's jammed, Hannibal!'

'What?' Hannbal turned his head to see what Peck's problem was. At the same time, one of the bikers a few men back of Snake let loose with a spare helmet that had fallen free during the pile-up. His aim was good enough for the helmet to come crashing down on Hannibal's forearm, forcing his hand to reflexively spring open. The automatic fell to the concrete and clattered through the bridge railing and down into the stream below. Before Hannibal could react further, Snake had whipped out his revolver and trained it on the van.

'Worm's turned, my man,' Snake laughed, pulling the trigger hammer back. Now you and your buddy with the burpgun better cool your heels or else I'm going to scratch your forehead with a .44, got it?'

'Loud and clear,' Hannibal said, staying put. In the back, Face was out of the biker's view, but there was little he could do but quietly tinker with the submachine gun in hopes he could get it working in time to use, provided such an opportunity would arise. Turning off the van's engine, BA hissed at Face, 'Did you release the safety, man?'

'Don't make me laugh,' Peck shot back. 'Of course I did. It's something else.'

While Snake kept the A-Team at bay, he ordered the other gang members to untangle their bikes and back out of the bridge, then head down the slope leading to the stream, which was shallow enough to cross. Several of the bikes had been damaged to the point where they couldn't be ridden, so their riders doubled up with other members. It took less than a minute for the whole manoeuvre to take place, leaving Snake alone on the bridge. He carefully mounted his cycle, then put his gun away, taunting, 'Okay, here's your big chance to get me!'

As Snake was turning his bike around, Hannibal took the bait and opened his door, bounding down to the pavement. When Snake roared off on his bike, though, Hannibal didn't run after him. Instead he rushed over to the side of the bridge and climbed up on the railing to wait for the biker to drive down the slope and across the stream below him. The drop was more than thirty feet, and before Hannibal had a chance to jump, BA scrambled out of the van and intercepted him, pulling him back from the railing.

'Don't be a fool, Hannibal! He ain't worth it, man!'

Hannibal tried to shake himself free, but BA's grip was like iron. Snake rode across the stream and up the other slope, rejoining the road and his companions, who were waiting for him.

'Let me go, BA, or you'll be sorry,' Hannibal warned. From the tone of his voice, BA knew the threat wasn't idle. He released his cohort, then followed as Hannibal strode back to the van, and squeezed past for one final look at the bikers. In the meantime, Peck had managed to get the submachine functioning, and he barrelled out of the van, dropping to a crouch and firing. A stream of bullets danced close to the bikers, and one managed to blow out the rear tyre of Snake's cycle. Enraged, Snake set the bike down and pulled his gun back out, returning the fire before leaping onto the back of a fellow member's chopper and shouting for the gang to resume its flight. Over the din of gunfire, the sound of wailing sirens was coming from the direction of Bad Rock, and new clouds of dust betrayed the coming of cops in hot pursuit.

'Well, we tried,' Hannibal sighed, watching the bikers retreat from view. 'Too bad I didn't have time to work on a better plan.'

'If this damn gun wouldn't have jammed, we would have had them,' Face grumbled, shaking the Thompson with annoyance. 'That's what we get for using antiques.'

As both men turned back to the van they broke into runs, seeing BA writhing on the pavement by the railing, holding both hands around his left leg.

'BA! What happened!' Face said as he reached the black man's side.

'I got hit, that's what happened, turkey!' BA said, grimacing with pain. 'When you shot at that dude, he fired back and got me!'

Hannibal crouched alongside BA and pulled the injured man's hand aside to inspect his wound. 'Nasty. You're bleeding pretty bad, BA, Stay put. Face, see if you can flag down somebody when the cops come.'

'Right.' Face put a hand on BA's shoulder and apologized, 'Hey, I'm sorry. Really.'

'I thought you said you never let me down, sucker!'

Face stood up and swallowed, trying to force some humour, 'Hey, BA, anybody ever tell you you're cute when '

'Get help, Peck, damn it!' Hannibal shouted.

Face wriggled his way past the van and waved his arms wildly at the squadron of patrol cars and police cycles howling onto the scene. Somebody mistook his gestures and fired a shot at him, forcing Peck to dive to the pavement. By the time he summoned the nerve to show himself again, the authorities had detourted from the bridge, following the cycle tracks leading down the dirt slope and across the stream. Not so much as one car or bike stayed behind. The full force spun its way up the other incline and back onto the road before resuming the chase, leaving the A-Team alone.

By the time Face rejoined his associates, BA was already starting to drift in and out of consciousness, sweating profusely and breathing in short bursts.

'We gotta get him to a doctor, quick,' Hannibal said, shifting his position so he could get a good hold on BA. 'Help me get him in the van, Face.'

'J ... just a scratch,' BA mumbled drowsily. 'I'm okay.'

'We aren't taking any chances, my friend,' Hannibal told BA as he and Face hefted him into the back of the van.

'I'll drive,' Face said, closing doors and making his way to the front seat. As he started up the engine and carefully backed up to the point where he could start going forward, Hannibal pried open a large first aid kit and began using a combination of cotton, gauze and elastic bandages to staunch the flow of blood from BA's leg. Face guided the van around the mangled bikes cluttering the bridge, then picked up speed.

'We'll be in Bad Rock in a couple minutes,' he said, craning his neck for a glimpse of Hannibal and BA in the rear-view mirror. 'How is he?'

'A whole lot better than you're gonna be, sucker,' BA said through his pain.

'C'mon, BA,' Hannibal urged, 'Stay quiet and try not to move. That's no mosquito bite you've got there.'

'Is he gonna be all right, Hannibal?' Face asked.

The dressing over BA's wound was already turning red. Hannibal sorted through the first aid kit and slapped a blood pressure cuff around BA's arm, then began pumping it up. 'I don't know,' he finally told Peck, reading off the numbers as he let go of the pump bulb. 'Blood pressure is ninety over thirty and probably dropping. Must have nicked an artery or something. He's going to need some blood.'

'Face gonna have to change his name,' BA blathered, half-delerious. 'Yeah, Broken Face ...'

'C'mon, BA,' Face pleaded, rounding a bend and flooring the accelerator on a length of straightaway marking the outskirts of town. 'It wasn't my fault.'

'You messed up, bad ... now ... gonna have to mess you up ... it's the law.' BA swallowed hard between phrases, trying to blink the feverish sweat from his eyes.

'Hannibal, will you talk to him?' Face pleaded.

'BA, shut up and rest, would you?' Hannibal said. 'You'll cool off once we get you to a doctor. You don't '

'Ain't coolin' off 'til I square it with the Faceman,' BA vowed, his voice weakening. 'An eye for an eye ...'

'Whatever happened to turning the other cheek?' Face wondered dismally. 'Look, it's not like I fouled up deliberately. I mean, if you woulda had the Thompson, BA, it woulda jammed on you, too, at first. And as for taking a shot at that slimeball, well, it was the thing to ... whoah, Nellie! Here we are! Hallejuiah!'

Face pumped the brakes lightly to slow down the van,

then turned off into the driveway adjacent to a simply-lettered sign that read: 'DR M SULLIVAN, STANDARD PRACTICE.'

Hannibal peered out the windshield and frowned. 'Where are we? That looks like a private residence to me, Face.'

'Well, check out the sign,' Face said, turning off the van. 'Maybe this is their idea of a house call . . .'

As Hannibal threw open the rear doors of the van and Face circled around to help, BA came to enough to try getting out on his own.

'Hey, easy, BA, let us do the work,' Hannibal told him. 'Save your strength.'

'Yeah,' BA relented, letting the other two men help him out. 'Save it for Face.'

'Oh brother,' Face groaned, sagging under the weight of the man between himself and Hannibal. Acting like human crutches, they supported BA as they made their way across the lawn to a prim-looking one-storey house. It looked more like a home for newlyweds than a medical building, and once they reached the doorstep and rang the bell, Hannibal remarked, 'I sure hope this isn't a false alarm. BA needs help, pronto.'

When there was no answer, Face closed a fist and prepared to knock. Before he made contact, though, a woman's voice called out to them from the other side of the door.

'Who is it?'

'We need a doctor!' Face shouted. 'It's an emergency!' Under his breath, he muttered, 'Please don't be paranoid, lady.'

The men heard the sound of a deadbolt being turned, then the door creaked open. An attractive woman in her late thirties peered out, then stepped back, opening the door as her gaze drifted past BA's sweating features and took in his bleeding leg. Hannibal and Face braced BA up and eased him into the front hallway.

'Is Dr Sullivan in?' Hannibal enquired.

'I'm Dr Sullivan,' the woman responded, tightening the sash around her nightgown. She looked like she'd just gotten up. BA looked her over through bleary eyes and shook his head.

'Ain't no lady sawbone's gonna work on me.'

'Ignore him,' Face told the woman. 'He's in shock.'

'Had a hunting accident,' Hannibal explained. 'He's been shot in the leg and he's losing a lot of blood, as you can see. Sorry about your floor.'

'Don't worry about it, Dr Sullivan said, bending over and gently pulling aside the dressing on BA's leg for a better look at the bullet wound. Straightening up, she pointed through a nearby door and ordered, 'Bring him in there.'

Dr Sullivan had converted the den into an examination room, equipped with a full range of medicinal and surgical supplies. Hannibal and Face helped BA onto a gurney, then stepped aside as Sullivan took a pair of scissors to BA's pants and the dressing on his leg. 'When did it happen?'

'Half an hour ago, max,' Hannibal said. 'Probably less.'

'Thank goodness for that,' the doctor said, checking her watch as she took BA's pulse.

'You can help him, can't you?' Face asked,

BA was still conscious. Stirring, he raised one hand and pointed at Peck, warning, 'You better hope so, sucker.'

'Strap him down,' Sullivan told Face and Hannibal.

'Gladly,' Peck said, reaching for the closest strap dangling from the sides of the gurney. As Dr Sullivan loaded a syringe with pain killer, Face leaned over his friend, trying to calm him with words. 'We're with you, buddy. You're gonna be okay. You are, man. I promise.'

BA glared up at Face and said, 'You better not promise, Face. You better pray ...'

Once BA was strapped in place, Dr Sullivan, told Hannibal and Face, 'Okay, now would you please wait outside while I tend to him? It's apt to be a while but I think I can save him.'

'Save him?' Face said, crestfallen. 'You mean it's that serious?'

'You're lucky you got him here when you did,' she replied, giving BA the injection. 'That's all I can tell you right now ...'

NINETEEN

When forty-five minutes passed without Dr Sullivan emerging from the examination room, Face got up from the living room sofa and began pacing. 'He's right, you know,' he told Hannibal, who was taking a last puff from his cigar before stubbing it out. 'It's my fault.'

'Oh, cut the pity party, Face,' Hannibal insisted. 'It's not your fault and you know it. It was a rough break, that's all. Live in the fast lane the way we do and sooner or later you come up on the wrong side of the odds.'

'Hannibal, you're not the one he wants to break up. It's me. Did you see the look in his eyes?'

Hannibal nodded. 'Yeah. Kinda scary, isn't it?'

'You have to talk him out of it.'

'Face, quit pacing or we're going to owe the lady a new carpet on top of everything else. Sit down before you start making *me* nervous.'

Peck slumped back on the sofa. 'You *will* talk to him, though, won't you?'

'Face, nobody can talk to BA if he's not in the mood for listening and you know it.' There was a remote control for the television on the commode next to Hannibal, and he turned the set on to a local news channel, hoping to get some information on the bust in Bad Rock. The screen was filled with different coloured hands, one flashing weather statistics, another updating sports action around the nation, and a third headlining upcoming shows on an affiliate station. As he jumped from station to station, Hannibal told Peck, 'Just give it some time. He'll cool off. Worst that could happen is he'll take a swing or two at you.'

'One ought to do it,' Face said. 'Well, I guess if he pulls through it'd be a small price to pay, right?'

'Relax, Face, for crying out loud!' Hannibal turned off the television and pulled out a fresh cigar to keep his hands busy. 'BA loves you, man. He told me himself.'

'The only thing he loves is being mean.'

Just then the door to the examination room opened and Dr Sullivan stepped out. She'd changed into a white dress with a matching smock that bore a few smears of blood. A stethoscope dangled around her neck like an amulet. The look on her face wasn't encouraging.

'How is he?' Hannibal asked.

'Not very good,' Sullivan told them. 'Your friend has a .44 calibre hole in his right leg. I had to tie off an artery and it took fifty stitches to close him up. What were you hunting anyway, elephants?'

'Quail,' Face alibied flimsily. 'You know, we told him not to go bird-hunting with a Magnum, but some guys won't listen.'

'A Magnum .44? That's a police weapon, isn't it?'

'Ah, yes, ma'am,' Face said, 'but not exclusively. I'll be the first to admit, though, that it's more appropriate for two hundred pound thugs than tiny quails. I just hope our buddy's learned his lesson ...'

Hannibal stood up, asking, 'When can we get him out of here, Doc? He has a job interview in LA ...'

Dr Sullivan put her hands on her hips and scowled at the two men before her. 'Maybe you gentlemen were too busy with your stand-up routine to hear me, but I said your friend is in a bad way. He needs blood, and I can't locate any AB negative in the area. It's a very unusual type.'

'He's a very unusual guy,' Face countered.

'There you go again,' Dr Sullivan said, doing little to hide her disgust at Peck's levity.

'Look, Doc,' Hannibal cut in. 'I know this is usually your end of the rope, but we'll get you the blood and then we're taking our friend out of here. It's a very important job.'

Sullivan held her ground. 'That man doesn't move until I say so. AB negative is a very rare type. It'll take some time before we can locate even a pint of it.'

'Well, we just happen to know a very rare guy with very rare blood.' Hannibal glanced over at Face.

'Me? Sorry, Hannibal, I'm B positive.'

'Guess again.'

'You?'

'You're narrowing it down, Face.'

'Murdock?' Face said.

'He's our boy,' Hannibal said.

'Why Murdock? Why couldn't it be someone else? Anyone else?'

'Who is this Murdock you're talking about?' Dr Sullivan interjected.

'An acquaintance of ours,' Hannibal told her. 'He's down in LA, but I'm sure we could get him up here by sundown. Will BA hold that long?'

'BA?'

'Your patient's nickname,' Hannibal explained. 'Short for Bad Attitude.'

'How appropriate,' Dr Sullivan said. 'Well, if he stay's put, I think he'd be okay that long. Let him go much after that and we're asking for trouble, though.'

'Don't worry, Murdock'll get here on time, I promise.'

'How?' Peck exclaimed. 'How are we gonna get him up here, Hannibal?'

'Amy'll have to do it,' Hannibal said. Moving over to the phone, he asked Dr Sullivan, 'May I?'

'Go ahead,' she replied. 'While you're calling, I have some things to take care of myself. Excuse me . . .' Dr Sullivan left the living room, going into the kitchen and closing the door behind her. Going over to the wall phone, she carefully picked up the receiver to listen in on the conversation between Hannibal and Amy.

'This is Amy, can I help '

'Amy, it's Hannibal.'

'Hannibal! Hi! I just talked to Simon and he told me you

missed most of the action. He said something about you being near where the bike gang was going to be making –'

'Amy, listen to me. We've run into some problems and we need Murdock. You're going to have to get him out of the VA and bring him up here, right away!'

'But, Hannibal. My story ... I've got to sort through all the notes Simon gave me and incorporate them into the –'

'It'll have to wait, Amy. We're talking about life and death here, do you understand?'

'What? What happened?'

'Just get Murdock and get up here. Then you can meet Commonble and get all the gory details in the flesh.'

'How do I get him? You mean run a con or something?'

'There's no time for that. We need him right away. Call Murdock and tell him this: 'Red Ball One; the bag is leaking.' He'll think of something and take it from there.'

'Won't you at least tell me what's wrong?'

'Just tell him, Amy! He'll know what to do. Here's the address we're at ...'

Dr Sullivan slowly hung up the phone, disturbed. She wasn't sure about the background of the men in the other room, but she was certain they hadn't just been out on a hunting expedition. She went over to the kitchen window and glanced out at the van, spotting a bullet hole in the vehicle's front side, near where BA had been standing when he'd been shot. Becoming more suspicious, she stole back to the kitchen door and leaned her ear against it. Once she could tell that Hannibal was off the phone and that both men were talking on the far side of the living room, she went back and picked up the receiver, then slowly dialled a local number. When there was an answer on the other end, she spoke in a low voice, so as not to be overheard.

'Jack?' This is Mo Sullivan. Is the Sheriff in?'

TWENTY

Bad Rock got its name and its fame from a massive boulder that had rolled downhill back in the days of the gold rush and flattened a stagecoach hauling mining agents to Sutter's Mill. The boulder was now the focal point of a Memorial Park located in the heart of the small town, which consisted primarily of a quarter-mile stretch of Main Steet, sided by small shops catering to a few hundred local residents and the occasional tourist that might wander through asking for directions to Nevada. Life was slow and easy in Bad Rock, where people liked to keep at least a few steps behind the times, finding little in current trends worth trying to catch up to. This was a town where the fine art of idle conversation flourished, where folks still liked to sit on benches outside the general store and gossip the day away. Today, of course, the town was all astir over the big to-do that had taken place earlier in the morning out at the trailer park just past the city limits. Word had spread quickly in the wake of the first gunshots fired during the bust, and embellishments were already painting the whole episode into an epic confrontation between good and evil that ranked right up there with the Archangel Michael and his loyal followers routing the hordes of Lucifer from Heaven's Gate. Rumour had it that the local constabulary now had in custody no less than the living embodiment of Satan himself, a motorcycle gang chieftain who had afforded his sinly ways by virtue of selling fair young maidens into the hands of those who ran the trailers of the damned outside the town. While the vast majority of other tales being spun about the altercation were the stuff of imaginative fancy, this one speculation was true, for Jenko Stark, leader of the scourged Road Warriors, was indeed behind bars in the Bad Rock City Jail.

There were only two cells in the jail, which was housed at the far end of Main Street. One was empty, having been vacated earlier in the morning by Frank Truey, the town drunk, who had used it overnight for lodging, as was his custom. Jenko was in the other, his gangly frame sprawled out on the cot that served as his bed. He had his hands folded behind his head as he stared vacantly at the light pouring through the barred cell window. His slovenly, mean-spirited appearance made his fellow gang members look almost debonair in contrast. Four days growth of ragged beard covered his face, barely concealing the scars he'd earned from a lifetime of brawling and hard living. He was missing a few teeth, and the ones he still had were stained and rotting. The one facial resemblance he shared with his older brother was in the eyes, which were of a grey, reptilian hue, protruding in their sockets like eggs laid in nests too small to hold them.

Watching over Jenko were two men as dissimilar in looks and bearing as the Stark brothers. Jack Harmson was pot-bellied and near-sighted, with thick jowls and a drooping moustache, wearing a deputy's uniform that threatened to burst any moment from the strain on its stitches. He was at his desk, talking on the phone as he engaged in his daily ritual of memorizing statistics on the sports page so that he could maintain his reputation at the Bad Rock Saloon once he was off-duty.

'Yeah, Mo, I'll get him.' Cupping his hands over the receiver, he called out, 'Sheriff? Doc Sullivan's on the horn.'

Hank Thompson had just turned forty. His hairline was receding, but a well-kept fitness regimen maintained the same physique that had enabled him to be an All-State quarterback two years running back in his college days. He was a stern man with no mood for nonsense. The towns-folk knew it, which was why the Bad Rock City Jail usually had at least one of its cells vacant. As deputy Harmson called out to him, Hank was setting a cup of fresh-brewed coffee into Jenko's cell.

'Answer your phone, scumball!' Jenko told the sheriff as he swung upright on the couch and got up to sample the coffee. 'You ain't got much time left to enjoy yourself, though, pig. No way the Warriors'll let you save their main man for the Feds.' The biker paused long enough to take a sip of coffee and spit it through the bars of his cell, barely missing Thompson. 'No way,' he laughed. 'You in it now, man. You in it bad.'

'Nodody's comin' back for you, punk,' Thompson replied, unperturbed by Jenko's outburst. He went over to the desk and took the receiver from Harmson. 'What's up, Mo?'

'Hank, I may have some trouble. Two men brought someone to my place this morning. He's been shot up pretty bad.'

Thompson turned his back to the cell and lowered his voice. 'Are they Road Warriors?'

'I don't know for sure, but the one who was shot. He's got a Mohawk, about two tons of gold and bad manners.'

'I'll be over in a couple of minutes,' Thompson said, hanging up the phone and quickly moving over to the rifle rack on the far wall. He unlocked a pair of shotguns, handing one to Harmson and keeping the other for himself. 'I'm going over to Doc Sullivan's,' he told the deputy. 'Nobody comes through that door but me.'

'Gotcha, boss,' Harmson replied, doing a bad job of hiding his sudden nervousness.

As Thompson headed for the door, Jenko called out, 'Hey, copper, you think I don't know what's goin' down? What'd I tell you? My boys are already on their way back to get me, right?'

'Guess again, Stark,' Thompson told him. 'You're staying here until there's room for you at county, then you'll be on the way to what you deserve.'

Thompson left the jail and hopped into the town's lone squad car. Deputy Harmson tried to concentrate on the sports page, but the looming presence of Jenko Stark in the cell across from him was now too much to ignore.

'You think that chump's gonna stand up to my boys? Man, we eat pig for breakfast!' Jenko let out another of his laughs, which sounded like they came from a hyena with glandular problems.

'Shut up!' Harmson warned him. 'I'm not in the mood for your yap.'

'You ain't gonna make it,' Jenko sniggered. 'You're runnin' outta time and I'm goin' home. Gettin' out and goin' home, Fatman. Maybe you oughts go buy yourself some doughnuts, man, 'cause it'll be your last meal ...'

Harmson tried to discreetly suck in his gut as he sat upright at his desk and scowled at his tormentor. 'Forget about it. Your gang ran scared and left you for dead. You're all alone. You and your mouth.'

'We'll see, pig. We'll just wait and see,' Jenko went back to his cot and laid down, then began laughing again. Harmon's flesh began to crawl. He drew the rifle closer to his side and suddenly found himself listening intently, half-expecting to momentarily hear the sound of approaching motorcycles.

TWENTY-ONE

Dr Sullivan checked in on BA for a few minutes before re-entering the living room. Face and Hannibal had both stopped talking and were fighting off the urge to nod off. When Sullivan cleared her throat to get their attention, both men became suddenly alert.

'Is our friend any better?' Hannibal asked.

The doctor nodded her head. 'He won't be, either, until that friend of yours gets up here and gives him some blood.'

Hannibal and Face glanced at one another. Face gave a slight nod and Hannibal rose to his feet. 'I know this is unusual, Doctor,' he said, 'but we have to ask for your confidence. No one can know about this. We'll pay you in cash and as soon as BA can be moved, we'll take him out of here. How much do you want?' He pulled out the cash they taken as payment from Ed Maloney and began flipping through fifty dollar bills. The supply seemed endless. 'A thousand? Two thousand?'

'I don't want a penny,' Dr Sullivan answered warily, glancing over Hannibal's shoulder out the front window. What she saw helped bolster her courage. Taking a deep breath, she demanded, 'I want to know what happened to my patient. I haven't seen wounds like that since Nam.'

Hannibal was taken aback, but only for a moment. Extending his palm for a handshake, he said, 'If you were in Nam that means you must've been a captain. You'll excuse me if I don't salute.'

'He was a colonel over there,' Face explained, getting up from the sofa.

'Oh, is that a fact?' Dr Sullivan said. 'How inter –'

Before she could finish her sentense, the front door swung open and Hank Thompson lurched into the house, brandishing his riot gun.

'Freeze it or lose it!' he commanded, levelling the weapon at Hannibal and Face, who quickly complied. 'Raise 'em real slow.'

'I think there's been some kind of mistake here,' Face said.

'Your mistake was coming here,' Thompson retorted. 'Mo, see if they have guns.'

Sullivan crossed the room and circled behind Hannibal frisking him until she came up with his Browning pistol. 'Nice automatic,' she commented, fitting the butt into her hand and holding the gun like she knew how to use it. Checking Face, she came up empty handed.

'I rely strictly on charm,' Face said, smiling.

'He's not armed,' Sullivan told Thompson, stepping back next to the sheriff.

'We're on a cold streak here,' Hannibal said, trading glances with his partner. 'No doubt about it.'

Thompson produced two sets of handcuffs and used them to link his prisoners' hands behind their backs before escorting them out to the squad car. Dr Sullivan followed, keeping the Browning trained on Hannibal and Peck.

'I'd go with you into town,' she told Thompson, 'but I have to keep an eye on their friend. There's also supposed to be at least two others coming up later in the day. One of them is giving blood for the guy that's injured.'

'I can handle these two,' Hank said. 'Once I'm back at the station I'll put a call through to Didelticrol and see if he can have some men drop by later, in case you need help with the newcomers.'

'Thanks, Hank.'

'No problem.'

Before Hannibal climbed into the back seat of the squad car, he looked back at Mo. 'I'm not too thrilled about this detour you've put us on, doc, but we appreciate the work you've done on BA. Once we clear up this misunderstanding, we'll be by to pick him up and settle our debts.'

'We'll see about that,' Thompson said, closing the door once Hannibal and Peck were inside, then circling around to the driver's side and getting in behind the wheel. As he pulled out of the driveway and headed for the jail, located only a mile down the road, he said over his shoulder, 'I don't know about your friend, but neither of you guys look like bikers to me, and I don't remember seeing you during the bust this morning. You want to come clean with me and save us all a lot of trouble?'

'The guy back with the doc is none other than Big Abe Genes, heavyweight wrestling champ of the whole damn southeast,' Face boasted, trying to keep a straight face. 'I'm his manager and this here's Abe's trainer. We were on our way to a big bout in Tahoe when we ran –'

'Save your breath with that one,' Thompson said. 'I had a peek at your van before I barged in. You've got LA plates on the outside and weapons galore inside. I didn't see any wrestling gear, and, what's more, the heavyweight wrestling champ of the whole damn southeast is Henry Guyot . . . my deputy's a nut about sports facts, and he hit me with that one just the other day.'

'Well, our man Abe just defeated Guyot less than two –'

'Forget it!' Thompson told Face as he pulled up in front of the jail and parked. 'Come up with something better for my deputy to put in his report.' Opening the door for Hannibal and Peck, he said, 'Better yet, why don't I just get your driver's licenses and save your imaginations?'

'Driver's licenses?' Hannibal said. 'Neither of us drive, officer. And as for any other i.d., well, as I was trying to tell you ways back, we were robbed and –'

'Funny, I seem to remember Mo pointing to a wad of bills in your pocket when she was frisking you,' Thompson said. As Hannibal got out of the car, the sheriff reached for the money in question and noted the denominations of the bills. 'Just which side of this robbery were you on, pal?'

'Never mind,' Hannibal said. Face got out next and Thompson herded the two men inside, ignoring the few townsfolk who were watching from a few storefronts down.

Inside the jail, Harmson greeted Thompson's return with open relief, then squinted at the prisoners. 'Hey, who are those guys?'

'The mystery guests,' Thomspon drawled, leading Hannibal and Face to a bench next to the main desk and gesturing for the men to sit down. 'They think it'd be fun for us to spend the next few hours guessing their real identities.'

'Don't guess that we're involved with wrestling,' Face said. 'It's already been used.'

The deputy rolled his eyes and sighed clearing off enough room on the desk for an arrest report and an ink pad, which he set near the prisoners just as Thompson was undoing their handcuffs. 'Finger painting time, boys. I'm sure you know how it's done.' As Face and Hannibal inked their fingertips and then pressed them onto the appropriate spaces in their arrest reports, Harmson remarked, 'We'll find out who you are when we run your prints.'

'Okay, okay,' Hannibal sighed begrudgingly as he wiped his fingers clean on a towel provided by Thompson. 'He's Marvin Gardens and I'm the King of Hearts. We're a dance troupe.'

'That guy over at Doc Sullivan's is our choreographer,' Face put in.

'We had trouble in a cold house just across the border. I guess they didn't like our duet. Started shootin' at us from the first row. Nasty business. Makes you long for the days when they just threw rotten vegetables ...'

Thompson's patience ran out and he grabbed Hannibal by the collar, pulling him up from the bench and escorting him over to the open cell. The sheriff was backing his actions up with a service revolver, and when the gun's barrel pointed at Face, he got up and joined Hannibal in the barred enclosure.

Jenko Stark had been watching the proceedings silently up to now, trying to hide his disappointment in finding it wasn't members of his gang that Thompson had gone out to fetch. He gradually reclaimed his cocky bravado, though, and gave his new suitemates a light round of applause, howling, 'All right, more dog meat for the party. Gonna have a big party, man, and you're invited.'

Face looked Jenko over, then surveyed the rest of the jail, observing, 'Nice little place you have here, Sheriff. Who's the two hundred pound cockroach?'

'Him?' Thompson said, locking the cell door. 'Jenko Stark. He's in even more trouble than you guys. Heads up a pack of dirtballs that just got taken out of the white slavery racket. I guess you could say he's a local celebrity. Lot of folks here would love to reinstate the gallows just to give him a chance to wear a necktie for a change.'

'Oh, funny, funny man!' Jenko razzed the sheriff. 'You ain't gonna get me to trial, pig. I got my whole gang comin' back to get me outta here. Wait and see.'

'You keep saying that,' Thompson sneered.

'Jenko Stark, eh?' Hannibal said, grinning at Face. 'Small world.'

Jenko looked over at Hannibal. 'What you talkin' about?'

'Oh, nothing,' Hannibal replied nonchalantly. 'Nothing at all . . .'

TWENTY-TWO

Amazing things, computers. Leaps and bounds in technology over the years have made this burgeoning new field the most influential phenomena in modern civilization since the discovery of breath mints. When you get right down to it, there's really not a whole hell of a lot that computers *can't* do. One of the grandest testimonials to the prowess of these fiesty bands of microchips and solder was instigated by Deputy Sheriff Jack Harmson of Bad Rock, California, when he drove to the highway patrol outpost in nearby Fair City and requested a desk sergeant there to run a check on the two sets of fingerprints he'd brought over from the Bad Rock City Jail. While Harmson was driving back to Bad Rock, where he was told he'd hear from the sergeant as soon as he had some information, the computers in Fair City were having intimate, chip-to-chip conversations with other computers in Sacramento, Los Angeles, Washington, DC, and Fort Bragg. They chatted back and forth, swapping old familiar stories, then conferred on the question at hand and finally reached an undisputed consensus. By the time Harmson walked into the Bad Rock jailhouse, licking from his lips the last tell-tale trace of frosting from the slice of German chocolate cake he'd wolfed down at Hegiger's Truck Stop on the way back, the phone was ringing with results from Fair City. Harmson let out a low whistle as he took down the information, then hung up the phone and turned to his boss, who was sitting at his own desk, catching up on the latest innovations in red tape devised by some sadistic bureaucrat in the state capitol.

'That was Fair City, Hank,' Harmson explained. 'They just got a positive i.d. on those prints from military intelligence. Our guests here are Colonel John Smith, also known as Hannibal Smith, and Lieutenant Templeton Peck, also known as The Face Man.'

'You're kidding! Thompson explained, gladly setting aside his paperwork. 'Never would have figured them for officers.'

'Their rank goes back a long way. There's a Colonel Lynch outta Fort Bragg that's been after these two bozos since after we pulled out of Viet Nam.'

'This gets more interesting all the time,' Thompson said. 'What'd they do?'

'Get this ... they robbed the Bank of Hanoi!'

Thompson glanced over to the far side of the room, where Face and Hannibal were huddled in the corner of their cell, absorbed in conversation. Jenko was back laying on his cot and staring out the window. The Sheriff shook his head and got up from his chair, muttering, 'Boy, we've got ourself a couple real acts on our hands, Jack, eh?'

'The military police are sending some men up late this afternoon to pick up Smith and Peck,' Harmson said. 'Too bad they can't haul Jenko away, too.'

'Amen to that,' Thompson agreed. 'He's enough to keep my hands full.'

'We better watch those other two real close, though. Military Intelligence said Smith ... he's the one with the white hair ... they said he's supposed to be some kind of escape artist or something. Broke out of Fort Bragg once already, along with Peck and a guy named Bosco Baracus. I got a feeling that's the guy up at Mo's.'

'No one breaks out of my jail,' Thompson vowed. He stuffed his hands into his pockets and idled over to the cells, coughing to get the prisoners' attention. 'So, we've got ourselves some hot shot brass, huh?' he mocked. 'John "Hannibal" Smith?'

'Congratulations,' Hannibal said drily, getting up and

walking over to face Thompson. 'You win a prize for coming up with that, Sheriff? I'm impressed.'.

'Come on, Colonel … the Bank of Hanoi?'

'Yeah,' Hannibal beamed. 'We kinda liked that one ourselves.'

From back in the corner, Face interjected, 'You could say we had a "yen" for some extra money.'

'Old, Face,' Hannibal said, shaking his head. 'That joke's on Medi-Care by now.'

'Sorry.'

'We'll you're finally going to get to have your day in court, gentlemen,' Thompson announced. 'We've got some MPs on their way up here to take you guys back home to the stockade.'

'No offence, Sheriff,' Hannibal said, 'But that's been tried before.'

'You're not breaking out of here, Smith,' Thompson said, testing the strength of the cell bars. 'They told us you and your boys already broke out of Fort Bragg. But my jail's different.'

'That's the understatement of the year,' Hannibal snorted, taking in his place of captivity with a look of amusement. 'I don't like to brag, Sheriff, but I could break out of this cush joint on horseback with a bad case of the flu.'

'I'll take my chances, Houdini.'

'The name's Hannibal.'

Peck wandered over to the confrontation and told Thompson, 'Maybe you'd like to put a little money down on the security around here, Sheriff? Me, I've seen Hannibal pick a lock with nothing more than an over-starched shirt collar and a broken button. Twenty dollars says he can spring himself outta here. I'll even let the dirtball next door hold the money.'

'What'd you call me?' Jenko blurted out, bounding from his cot to the bars separating the two cells.

'I think he called you a dirtball, Jenko,' Hannibal told him. 'Dirtball, scumball … some kinda oddball at any rate.'

Jenko shook his head, fuming. 'You got a real mouth on you, punk. The both of yas. When my boys come to get me outta here, I'm gonna shut 'em myself.'

'You're expecting company?' Hannibal enquired. 'Gee, maybe I'll stick around. I haven't partied in days ...'

'Nobody's coming back for that creep,' Thompson said. 'His gang's long gone. And you're not going anywhere either, Colonel.'

As Thompson headed back to his desk, Hannibal hounded him. 'Hey, Sheriff, never underestimate your enemy. Too much confidence can be a real killer ... I think General Custer said that. At least he should have.'

'Don't worry about me, Smith,' Thompson called out, settling back in behind his desk. 'You just worry about what you're gonna tell that military court when they send you up for life.'

'I never worry,' Hannibal said. 'Bad for the body, bad for the soul.'

As Thompson waded back into his paperwork and Harmson busied himself with the sports page, Hannibal looked over at Jenko and said, 'What makes you think your gang will come back for you, ace? We ran into them on their way out of town, and they didn't look like they were in a real hurry to come back. What's more, they didn't look like they were that hard up for someone to give the orders while you're away ...'

'You're jivin' me, man,' Jenko said. 'I ain't listenin', got it? They'll come back for me. See, I'm the only one who's got access to the last batch of cash we got before the bust. If they want their slice, it's gotta come from me.'

'Clever man,' Hannibal told him. 'That's what I call a real incentive plan ...'

TWENTY-THREE

Howling Mad Murdock's most recent departure from the Veteran's Administration Hospital had been achieved with a bit less finesse than previous escapes. There was no member of the A-Team dropping by in some elaborate disguise to unveil a preposterous pretext for Murdock's release. He didn't disguise himself and slip out the door as someone else, either. Instead, after getting a call from Amy containing the buzz words 'red bag one, the bag is leaking', Murdock had merely complained to his nurse about feelings of claustrophobia and a need for some fresh air. He'd been taken outside to watch the afternoon croquet finals between the nurses and the orderlies, and as soon as he'd seen Amy pull into the parking lot, Murdock had bolted from his nurse's side and outraced a group of pursuing orderlies to the car. Amy had floored the accelerator and, *viola*, Murdock was on the loose again.

Because time was of the essence, Amy had nixed her original plans to drive up to Bad Rock and had instead booked seats for her and Murdock on a noon flight out of LA International to Sacramento, saving them four hours. At the state capitol, they had rented a car and headed east. By the time the gas gauge was flirting with empty, it was only a little past three o'clock and they were coming up on a vast stretch of National Forest that marked the halfway point to their destination.

Pulling into a service station, Murdock told Amy, 'You

136

can powder your nose while I handle the hose.'

'You're doing it again, Murdock,' Amy groaned, getting out of the car and stretching.

'Doing what, buttercup?'

'That infernal rhyming,' Amy said. 'You've been doing it all the way up here. Honestly, I feel like I'm travelling with Mother Goose.'

'I'm sure it's just a short-term phase,' Murdock replied as he manned the pump and started filling the tank with regular. 'Won't last more than a couple days.'

'Well, see if you can't phase it out while I'm gone,' Amy sighed, heading off to pay for the gas and use the rest room.

'I'll tend to the gas, and I won't give no sass,' Murdock said once she as beyond earshot. Glancing around at the surrounding, he began whistling to himself.

The first stand of hearty pines was only a few hundred yards away, dotting the foothills that marked the fringe of the forest. As Murdock watched on, a single figure emerged from the woods astride a motorcycle. It wasn't a dirt bike, though, but rather a customized chopper. Then, one by one, fourteen other riders roared out of the wilderness and followed their leader down a dirt road that eventually led to the service station. It was Snake and the other members of the Road Warriors, emerging from the woodland they'd taken refuge in while shaking the authorities that had chased them out of Bad Rock. Their bikes were covered with dust, dirt, and pine needles, and the men weren't any cleaner. They pulled into the station just as Murdock was putting the nozzle back and Amy was stepping out of the rest room.

Amy's sudden appearance was greeted by a chorus of wolf whistles and cat calls from the Warriors, who circled around the service island like Indians on the warpath, blocking her path to the car.

'My, my my,' one of the bikers murmured, licking his lips as he ogled Amy. 'Ain't you a pretty one, though. Why don't you hop on board and we'll go for a little ride, eh?'

Amy shot the man a withering gaze and squeezed past his bike and the one ridden by Snake.

'Hey,' Snake called out, loud enough for all to hear, 'We

got ourselves a hot shot high society lady here!'

'Would you gentlemen please leave me alone?' Amy asked calmly as she headed for the car, where Murdock was holding the door open for her and keeping an eye on the bikers.

'Aw, gee, the lady doesn't want anything to do with us,' Snake moaned to his men. 'What do you guys think of that?'

As the other Warriors let out more whoops and seasoned them with a few evocative profanities, Amy slid over into the driver's seat and started the engine, hissing out to Murdock, 'Come on, let's get out of here while we can.'

'In a moment, pet,' Murdock told her, staying outside the car. 'I'm not done yet.'

'Great!' Amy muttered. 'My life's on the line and my only ally's a poet.'

'Hey!' Snake shouted at Murdock over the rumble of motorcycle engines. 'Is your momma too cool to ride with us, beanpole? Maybe we oughta change her mind.'

Murdock cleared his throat, then boldly recited,

'In the midst of prose and song,
I find the road is long.
But with guys like you,
It could only be true,
In a zoo is where you belong ...'

'Murdock, get in here!' Amy said, revving the engine and leaning across the front seat to grab him by the belt.

She tugged hard and he got the message, sitting down and pulling the door shut as Amy raced forward, veering the car sharply to one side and rushing past a break in the circle formed by the bikers. They responded by throwing beer cans and other bits of litter snatched up from the asphalt, but before any of them could take off in pursuit, Snake yelled out, 'Let 'em go! We don't have time for 'em. Let's get our gas and head back to Bad Rock ...!'

TWENTY-FOUR

Sheriff Thompson hung up the phone and told his deputy, 'Doc Sullivan is still trying to locate some blood for the guy that got shot up. As soon as he's stabilized, we'll move him in here and hold him for the MPs.'

Harmson was loading a serving tray with meals for the prisoners. His back was turned to Thompson and the cells on the far side of the room. 'What time the Feds coming for Stark?'

'Depends on how fast they can process all the other guys they hauled into county,' Thompson said. 'Maybe tonight. No later than tomorrow morning, I'd imagine. Think your nerves'll hold out that long, Jack?'

'I don't know,' the deputy replied, dabbing a single tea bag into three separate cups of hot water. 'It's a little too quiet for my taste. I figure we would've heard more on what's happened to the Road Warriors by now, one way or the other. They didn't run off into the woods to play Robin Hood and his Merry Men, especially with their Hood in our slammer. I just got this feeling they're gonna try and sneak back, at least to throw some rocks through our windows or something.'

'The Warriors are punks, they don't have the guts.' Thompson said. 'Listen, while you're over there, you think you could pour me a cup of coffee?'

Harmson filled the sheriff's mug and brought it over on the tray, balancing the full load of meals and drinks with considerable effort. As Thompson reached for his coffee, Harmson told him, 'I hope you're right ... about the Warriors, that is.'

Thompson blew across the brim of his cup, staring abstractly at the brown ripples raised by his breath. 'Yeah, I hope I'm right, too,' he murmured.

Carrying the tray across the room to the cells, Harmson called out, 'Feeding time at the zoo, fellas.'

Jenko rolled over on his cot and grumbled, 'If this is a zoo, then the food must be for you, pig!'

'You're a real card, Jenko,' Harmson drawled, setting the biker's rations through the bars of his cell door. 'Too bad you're bound for the state pen or you might have been able to sub for Carson on the Tonight Show.'

'Hey, that's a good one, deputy,' Face called out in the next cell. 'Really. I mean it.'

'Save the flattery for your lawyer, Peck,' Harmson said.

'There's another one!' Face gasped. 'You're on a roll, Harmson. Don't stop now.'

The deputy blushed in spite of himself as he slipped the remaining two meals into the other cell. Face stayed put on his cot, watching Harmson with a look of amusement. Hannibal was curled up in his bed, covered completely by a blanket that extended all the way to the floor.

'C'mon, Colonel, wake up. Lunch time.' When Hannibal didn't respond, Harmson clanged his keys against the bars and raised his voice. 'I said wake up!'

'Save your breath, deputy,' Face told him. 'He's gone. You're talking to a decoy. He plumped his pillows –'

'Hey, Sheriff!' Harmson yelped, a frantic rage coming over him as he fumbled through his keys for the one that opened the cell. By the time Thompson had circled around his desk and joined him, the deputy had the door open and was rushing over to Hannibal's cot, pulling down the blanket as he drew his gun.

'Damn!' Thompson swore, staring over Harmson's shoulder at the pillows that had been positioned on the cot to simulate the contours of a sleeping man.

Face smirked at the gaping man. 'He just stepped out for a

cheeseburger down the block. I'm sure he'll be back –'

Thompson pulled out his service revolver and charged out of the cell, shouting, 'Let's go!'

Harmson hesitated a moment, staring at the cot. 'But how –'

'Come on, Harmson! I want him caught and back here before the MPs arrive,' Thompson fumed. 'No one breaks out of my jail!'

'Seems to me you owe me twenty bucks, Sheriff,' Face said, but both officers were already on their way out the door, where they headed off in separate directions, eyes alert for the escaped prisoner. At that moment, however, Hannibal hadn't yet escaped. Pushing his cot out from the wall, the Colonel got up from the floor, dusting himself off.

'Nice work, Hannibal.'

'Thanks, Face,' Hannibal said. 'Now, since you bet they wouldn't fall for it, you're the one who owes *me* twenty bucks.'

'Put it on my tab.'

Realizing what Hannibal had done, Jenko called out from his cell, 'Hey, good move, whitehead! Those morons didn't even bother to lock your door, they were in such a hurry. Get out and see if you can find another set of –'

'Cool it, ace,' Hannibal told Jenko as he strolled out of the cell and grabbed one of the riot guns from the rifle rack. 'I'm not in your club, remember? I don't have to kiss your ring and I don't plan to ...'

Hannibal had just helped himself to one of the cigars resting on Thompson's desk when the sheriff and deputy rushed back inside, caught up in flurried conversation.

'Start up the squad car,' Thompson was saying, 'I'll put a call through to the state police and ... Smith!'

Both officers ground to a halt at the sight of the twin rifle bores aimed at their midsections. 'No need to make that call now, Sheriff,' Hannibal said as he popped the cigar in his mouth. 'They serve real fast food at that stand down the block. I beat you back.'

'You won't get away with this,' Harmson threatened.

'I sure aim to try.' Hannibal eyed the men's guns. 'Now,

drop your pea-shooters real slow and easy. Harmson, toss my friend the keys to the car.'

Thompson and Harmson warily complied. As he was throwing Face the keys, the deputy asked Hannibal, 'How did you –'

'Claustrophobia,' Hannibal cut on. 'Tight places give me the creeps.'

'You're just racking up more felonies by the minute, Colonel,' Thompson advised Hannibal. 'Give it up while you still can.'

Hannibal shook his head and pointed to the cell he and Face had just vacated. 'C'mon, move inside, boys. It's the best room we've got. By the week or by the month. No phone, no pool, no pets, but you're gonna love your new neighbour.'

'Hold on, my man!' Jenko said to Hannibal. 'Let's be cool here. We're both brothers on the lam, right? You let me out, I'll make sure you get a motorcycle escort to the state line.'

'No deal,' Hannibal told Jenko as he locked Thompson and Harmson into their cell. 'I couldn't stand the smell. Besides, I don't think you're smart enough to find the state line with a tour guide.'

Jenko threw himself against the bars, boiling with fury. 'You're gonna pay for that one, whitehead! I'll feed you your tongue on a sandwich for that! You'll pay, do you hear me?!!'

'Yeah, right. I'll cut you a cheque as soon as I get to the bank.' Hannibal turned his back on Jenko and looked in through the bars at Thompson. 'Sorry, Sheriff, but we don't get on well with the military police. They're holding an old grudge, as you already know. As soon as we're out of town I'll drop the keys somewhere and have the good doctor come and let you out.'

'You'll never get out of this one, Smith. The Feds are coming and so are the MPs,' Thompson said. 'You'll never make it out of the county.'

'Maybe, but if I didn't try, I wouldn't feel right about it.' Hannibal paused to light his cigar, then continued, 'They say it stems from my childhood. You see, I have this real need to play against the house.'

As the two mmbers of the A-Team headed for the door, Face glanced back at Jenko and waved. 'Take it easy, Lizard teeth. maybe you and your brother'll be bunkmates on Soledad once he gets out of the hospital ...'

'What are you talkin' about, man?' Jenko shouted. 'You keep mentionin' my brother. What's this about the hospital?'

'You're not in a position to send flowers, so don't worry about it,' Hannibal said. 'Ciao!'

Outside, there was no one watching on, so Hannibal and Face hustled into the squad car and quickly left the town behind. Face drove while Hannibal kept his eyes open for a possible glimpse of either Amy and Murdock or the military police. The only other traffic on the road, however, was a farm truck loaded down with bales of hay. Face flashed the rooflights and sped past, then slowed down and turned off into Dr Sullivan's driveway, parking behind their un-attended van.

'See if you can raise Amy or Murdock on the radio,' Hannibal told Face as they got out of the car. 'I'll go try to soften up Doc Sullivan before she can phone the heat.'

As Face let himself into the van and began fidgeting with the c.b. controls, Hannibal traded the rifle for a less conspicuous handgun and then stole around to the side entrance to Sullivan's house. The door there was locked, but he had better luck in back, gaining access through an open kitchen window. He moved with stealthy prowess, making only the slightest of sounds as he eased across the tiled floor to the examining room. He paused outside the half-opened door, spotting the doctor at BA's side, changing the wounded man's dressing as he writhed on the gurney.

'How do you feel?' she asked.

'Feel pretty weak, momma,' BA whispered hoarsely. Sweat was still beading up on his face.

'As soon as you get some blood you'll start getting some strength back,' the doctor told him. As she finished securing the fresh dressing, Sullivan turned away from BA, spotting Hannibal as he stepped into the room.

'Hi, Doc.'

'What are you doing here?' Sullivan said, trying to keep

down the surge of fear that had just shot through her. 'You're supposed to be in jail.'

Hannibal beat her to the phone and jerked its cord free from the wall. He'd tucked the gun under his belt, but he pulled the front of his jacket to one side so that Sullivan could see it. 'Sorry, Doctor, but we're going to have to do this my way. Don't worry, we're not going to hurt you.'

'What did you do to Sheriff Thompson and his Deputy?' Sullivan demanded.

'Realx. They're just going to spend a night in jail for disturbing my peace of mind, that's all.' Hannibal moved over to the gurney and put a hand on his partner's shoulder, asking him, 'BA, you hangin' in there?'

'Real tired, Hannibal,' BA groaned. 'And my leg hurts bad.'

'We're going to get you home real soon, pal.'

Dr Sullivan strode over, ignoring the presence of Hannibal's gun in her anger. 'This man cannot be moved until he gets some blood. I thought I made that clear before you were taken into custody. Nothing's changed since then, damn it!'

'Hey, Doc, get the fire out of your eyes, would you?' Hannibal said. 'We've got some on the way.'

BA feebly raised his head, managing a slight smile. 'Hannibal always comes through.'

'Yeah, Murdock should be almost here by now.'

'Murdock?' The smile left BA's face, replaced by a look of astonishment on its way to a scowl.

'You and Murdock have the same blood type, remember?' Hannibal said. 'We do a direct transfusion and get you back on your feet, pure and simple. Paint by numbers.'

'Murdock!!' BA mouthed the name like an anti-mantra, making him more agitated with each repetition. 'I ain't swappin' blood with that sucker, man. He's a total burnout.'

'Now, BA, it's the only donor we can find without admitting you to Cedars Sinai...you have very special blood.'

BA struggled to sit up, and Hannibal needed Sullivan's help to hold him down. 'Ain't gonna let you pump any of

Murdock's crazy juice into me, fool!' BA growled through his pain. 'No way. That man's crazy.'

'No he isn't, BA' Hannibal said half-heartedly. 'Not really...'

TWENTY-FIVE

The dashboard radio was blaring, and Murdock bobbed his head frantically in time with the music as he guided the sedan around the curving interstate. Amy sat next to him, a map spread out across her lap as she tried to concentrate on her navigating. The distractions going on around her proved to be too much, though, and she finally reached over and snapped off the radio. Murdock's head continued to bob for a few seconds, anticipating the beat of the silenced tune.

'Earth to Murdock,' Amy said, snapping her fingers. 'We're within miles of our destination. Please extinguish all theatrics . . .'

Murdock calmed down visibly, but he continued to hum the last few bars of the song under his breath. They'd left the national forest behind a few moments ago and were now passing along the outskirts of Fair City. Once she found her bearings on the map and saw that Murdock had calmed down, Amy said, 'What do you think went wrong?'

Murdock shrugged his shoulders. 'Dunno, but it's a red ball one, which means big trouble. The bag's leaking tells us one of the team took some lead.'

'It couldn't have been Hannibal,' Amy guessed. 'He made the call.'

'Nope, Hannibal ain't the one who's under the gun,' Murdock rhymed, pointing beneath the seat. 'Gimme the radio, hot patato . . .'

Amy withdrew the c.b. radio she'd brought along and set it

146

on the seat next to Murdock. He'd already wired it up, and he picked up the microphone as he drove. 'We should be in range pretty soon. Shootin' it out at high noon. Maybe we can raise the van, pull the A-Team out of the can.' Amy rolled her eyes, then cringed as Murdock activated the transmitter and began blabbering like a lobotomized Wolfman Jack. 'Howling Mad Murdock flyin' high cover on the red ball one... I'm coming in low and sideways to plug the bag. Hold your mud, I'm lost in the flood. A-Team in need, can you read?' When no response was forthcoming through the sea of static on the receiver, Murdock frowned. 'Outta range. Kinda strange...'

'Murdock, what's with all the poetry?' Amy said, exasperated. 'Can't you put a lid on it? Pretty please?'

'I try to ma'am, but I'm in a jam,' Murdock said. 'Got my words, and my brain's working fine, but whenever they come out, they want to rhyme.'

'Oh, brother...'

As they rounded the next turn and Amy pointed out the intersection leading into Bad Rock, a voice finally sputtered over the c.b. 'Murdock, is that you? Come in.'

Murdock's face lit up as he brought the mike back to his mouth. 'It's your man, Howlin' Mad... what's the buzz, Faceman?'

'BA's been hit... He needs some of your AB negative. The doc's place is a house on your right as you're heading into town. I'll be waiting for you...'

Driving along, Murdock spotted the A-Team van and the parked squad car in front of Dr Sullivan's residence. He yipped over the radio, 'No need to wait, Face. I think this is the place.'

The driveway was full, so Murdock parked on the shoulder in front of the house, then he and Amy rushed out to join Face.

'He's inside,' Face said as the three of them headed for the door. 'Murdock, roll up your sleeve. You're not a minute too soon.'

Inside the examination room, BA was strapped down to the gurney, barely stirring. Hannibal was dabbing the wounded man's perspiring brow with a damp cloth while Dr Sullivan took another test of BA's blood pressure. It was clear from the look on her face that she didn't like the results.

'Have no fear, the blood man's here,' Murdock announced as he swept into the room, followed by Amy and Face.

'Murdock!' Hannibal exclaimed with relief. 'All right!'

'Get that fool outta here!' BA wheezed. 'Better to give me red kool-aid than his juice, man.'

Dr Sullivan hurriedly rolled another gurney into position next to BA and began readying the necessary equipment for a transfusion. She asked Murdock, 'Are you absolutely certain your blood is AB negative? I don't have time to check.'

'Yes, ma'am, I am,' Murdock professed, laying down on the gurney and grinning across at BA, who resumed his weak attempts to get away. Hannibal and Face both held him down.

'C'mon, BA, don't move,' Hannibal told him.

'Don't put that sucker's blood into me ... gonna make me crazy just like he is ...'

As Dr Sullivan readied the pump and tubes that would allow for the transfusion, Murdock tried to calm BA 'It don't make you crazy, BA It just makes you mellow. Hell, man, you can even room with me at the VA I'll have 'em move in an extra bunk and you and I can watch the walls melt ...'

'Hannibal!' BA moaned desparately.

'Lay off him, Murdock,' Hannibal ordered.

'Lay off what?' Murdock winced as the doctor tapped an artery and started his blood pumping out of his arm and into BA's. 'This man's got a chance at greatness. My bodily fluids are in great demand by the finest minds of our time. I give a fresh specimen to the VA every week, without fail.'

'All right, Murdock,' Amy intervened. 'Enough. Just rest and let's get BA better, okay?'

'Worst that could happen is he starts to hear things he don't see,' Murdock rambled on, 'and rhyme his words just like me.'

'Murdock, shut up!' Hannibal said. 'That's an order!'

Murdock fell silent and watched his blood course through

the clear plastic tube into BA's arm. BA craned his head enough to see what was happening, too, then lay back, bitterly resigned to the transfusion. His gaze fell on Peck and darkened.

'I'm going to get you for this, Face.'

'Get him for what, BA?' Amy asked.

'Face messed up, that's why I got shot...' BA whispered angrily. 'That's why I need the blood... the blood's gonna make me crazy... I'm gonna make the Faceman pay.'

Peck motioned for Amy to take his place holding BA down, then backed away from the table. 'I think I'll go move the squad car out of the van's way, then get things ready to roll. Hannibal, please try to cool him down for me...'

'Don't worry,' Murdock called out, 'My blood's gonna cool him out for you, Face.'

'Yeah, right,' Face said dubiously, leaving the room.

Whether or not it was due to Murdock's blood, BA *did* cool off. Halfway through receiving his second unit of AB negative, the wounded man closed his eyes and began to snore.

'Is that normal?' Hannibal asked worriedly.

'He's been through a lot,' Dr Sullivan said. 'All thing's considered, it's probably the best thing he could do. I'd recommend the same course for you, Mr Murdock, since you're giving more blood than would normally be asked for.'

But Murdock wasn't listening to her advice. He, too, was lulling off into dreamland, a weird smile twisted upon his lips.

'Bloodbrothers,' Hannibal said, looking at them. 'I knew they'd draw closer together in time...'

TWENTY-SIX

BA awoke feeling rejuvenated, but he still wasn't strong enough to put up more than token resistance as he felt himself being wheeled outside the side entrance of Dr Sullivan's and down the driveway to the waiting van. Amy and Murdock were on either side of him, concentrating on keeping the gurney from crabbing sideways.

'Lemme off this thing!' BA said, fighting against his binds. 'I ain't a damn cripple!'

'Be careful, BA,' Amy advised him. 'You shouldn't even be moving this much.'

Face was at the van, opening the back doors and clearing the way for BA to be hoisted aboard. He looked at BA uncertainly, hoping to find a less disagreeable countenance than the one that had chased him out of the examination room less than an hour before. No such luck.

'Gonna get you for this, Face,' BA promised. 'I can feel myself gettin' crazy already.'

Murdock's rest had done little to abate his giddiness. If anything, the loss of blood seemed to have affected his brain more than anything else. As he helped Face and Amy jockey the gurney up into the van, he counseled BA 'Yeah, the first thing that happens is your ears start to ring. And then, every once in a while your eyes start to fog and you'll start rhyming your words...'

'You're nuts, man,' BA said. 'Rhymin' my words, that's the craziest thing I ever heard... My ears don't ring... I don't hear a... a... a thing.'

'I hate to say it, BA,' Amy said, 'But you just –'

'Hey!' BA roared, realizing what he'd just done. He jerked one arm forward in a fit of frenzy, ripping loose the strap that had been holding it down. His hand lashed out at Murdock like the head of an angry serpent. 'Wait a second, sucker!'

Fortunately for Murdock, BA's reactions weren't swift enough, and he was able to reel away from the grasping, bejewelled fingers before they closed around his jacket. 'You see?' Murdock cried out, springing back down to the asphalt. 'Foam the runways, BA's coming in. Let me know when your eyes start to fog, good buddy.'

Face reached out with one foot and closed the rear doors on Murdock, then turned his attention to BA 'Murdock's blood isn't going to do a thing to you, and you know it. Blood is blood. It's all the same. You know, red.'

Murdock poked his head in the side door, startling Amy. 'No, it ain't,' he insisted. 'Once upon a time, I didn't have a dime. My head went crazy, they said I was lazy. But I'm getting by, on the fly...!'

'Will you get off that poetry kick, Murdock?' Face pleaded. 'You're putting me in a real hole with BA here.'

'Rock and roll,' Murdock rhymed, unrepentant.

'It's okay, Face,' Amy said, pushing the side door open and climbing out. 'I've gotten used to it. I'll go with Murdock in the sedan and we'll follow you. Where's Hannibal anyway?'

'Tying up some loose ends, I believe,' Face said.

'I can imagine,' Amy said dryly.

Back inside the house, Hannibal was standing close to Dr Sullivan as the two of them sipped cups of coffee. She had relaxed slightly over the past hour, and there was even an inkling of romance brewing in the air, taking shape behind the last few shreds of antagonism between them.

'You shouldn't be moving him,' she said in tone that conceded that her opinions weren't about to sway the day.

'We don't have a choice, Doctor,' Hannibal said. He finished his coffee and stepped away from the wall he'd been leaning against, lost on a train of thought. Finally he turned to Sullivan and told her, 'Look, you're not going to believe this, but we're the guys with the white hats.'

'You're right,' Dr Sullivan replied. 'But, just for the sake of argument –'

'Wonderful,' Hannibal broke in, grinning. 'I just love a good argument.'

'If you're the good guys,' Sullivan went on, 'then why are you wanted by the military police?'

'Let's just say it's a long story and a big mistake on somebody else's part. But for now, nobody wants to listen to the truth, so we have to live on the run.'

Dr Sullivan set down her cup and looked up at Hannibal, coaxing a faint twinkle into her eyes. 'Sounds intriguing.'

'It's not a bad way to go,' Hannibal confessed, 'But the food stinks.'

'You're breaking my heart,' she smirked.

'No I'm not,' Hannibal said, drawing a step closer and putting a sparkle into his own gaze as he met the doctor's eyes. 'But, you know, given another time and place, I might like to try.'

Dr Sullivan let out an uncomfortable snicker, then retreated promptly to the safer ground of cynicism. 'That's supposed to be some kind of macho pass, and I'm supposed to blush, right?'

'No, you're supposed to say thank you,' Hannibal responded matter-of-factly. 'And I don't make passes.'

'Or promises.' Sullivan looked away, as if peering out the window into the distance. 'The mystery man just rides off into the sunset like the last reel of "Happy Trails" . . .'

'Something like that, yeah.' Hannibal moved another step closer. One more and they'd be colliding. He leaned his head forward. She tilted hers back and slowly closed her eyes, awaiting a kiss. It never came. 'But for now,' Hannibal whispered, reaching out suddenly and pushing Sullivan into the supply closet behind her, 'it's gonna have to wait!'

Hannibal swung the door shut and locked it. As he turned and headed for the door, there came a furious pounding from inside the closet as the doctor shouted, 'Hey, let me out of here! Damn you, Hannibal Smith!'

'Now, now,' Hannibal shouted back. 'We'll stop at a gas station and drop off the keys to the Sheriff's jail and tell them to have Thompson come let you out when he picks up their car. Sorry it had to be like this, Doc, but sometimes we have to rig the game.'

'You'll pay for this, mister! You'll pay!' Dr Sullivan raged between pummelings of the doorskin.

'That's the second time I've had someone tell me that in the past couple hours,' Hannibal commented. 'In your case, though, I think I'll oblige, Doctor.' Reaching into his pocket, he removed a few fifty dollar bills and set them on the surgical tray by the door. 'There's three hundred dollars here for you. I'd leave more, but we have to watch our cash flow until our next job is lined up. Besides, BA can't draw disability pay. I'm sure you understand.'

Sullivan's reaction was far from understanding, and Hannibal walked out on the barage of muffled profanity, joining Face in the front of the van. Glancing into the back, he asked BA, 'How you doin', big guy? Gonna pull through for us?'

'Ain't talking, Hannibal.'

As he started up the engine and drove off, Face explained to Hannibal, 'BA's afraid if he talks he'll start babbling in rhymes like Murdock.'

'I see.' Hannibal peered into the rear-view mirror and saw the rental sedan following a few lengths behind the van. Picking up the radio microphone, he pressed the speak button. 'Murdock?'

'Yeah, Colonel?'

'When we got busted, the Sheriff called us in to the military police. They could be on us any time. If you see any heat closing in, I want you to peel off and take Amy out of it. In any event, why don't you swing into town and try to track down Commonble? Amy might be '

'Hannibal!' Amy's voice suddenly sounded over the radio. 'If I'm on the team I see this whole thing through. My story can wait another day, and I want to -'

'As I've said before, Amy,' Hannibal reminded her, 'If

you're on the team, you take orders.'

'Am I getting to love that stuff?' Amy retorted.

Murdock's voice came back on, crowding out Amy's protests. 'You're in the army now, you're not behind the plough. You'll never get rich by digging a ditch. You're in the Army now.'

Hannibal clicked off the radio and mumbled, 'I'm getting worried about Murdock.'

'Hey, I've been worried about him for ten years,' Face said. 'Where have you been?'

They drove on quietly for a few more miles, putting Bad Rock behind them. Then Face said, 'What if that slimeball's back at the jail's right and his gang's really coming back to bust him out?'

'I wouldn't count on it,' Hannibal said, enjoying the scenery. 'My guess is the Road Warriors probably aren't within a hundred miles of here by now.'

TWENTY-SEVEN

Hannibal was only off by ninety-five miles.

The Road Warriors were halfway between Fair City and Bad Rock, travelling a back road that linked the two cities. On Snake's signal, they pulled off onto the shoulder to rest momentarily and tend to one of the last preliminary details prior to their seige of Bad Rock. As the others dismounted their bikes and stretched to work out the kinks in the backs from the long ride that had brought them this far, one of the gang members unlashed a chain saw from the back of his bike and started it up. The high-pitched whine of the saw's motor contrasted sharply with the deeper roars of the idling cycles. Snake scanned the rigid telephone poles lining the side of the road and pointed to the one that seemed to carry the most important load of wires and transmitters.

'That one,' he shouted to his crony. 'Cut it down!'

With a savage grin, the other biker waded through the weeds and approached the pole. After looking for an ideal spot, he closed in with the chainsaw and let its whirring teeth rip into the wood. Sawdust and splinters showered in a wide arc as the slice went deeper and deeper. Stopping halfway into the pole, the biker yanked the saw out and put it to work on the other side.

'Atta boy, Driver!' one of his companions rooted. 'Make like a lumberjack and bring that mother down!'

As the two indentations in the pole drew closer together, Driver was barely able to hear the first tell-tale creak warning him that he'd done enough sawing. He gave the saw one last thrust, then pulled it free and quickly ran clear as the pole swayed faintly to one side, allowing the displaced weight to sever the last few inches of solid wood holding it upright. With a loud, crunching sound, the pole toppled to the ground, snapping loose the cables it had been supporting. High power wires shot off sparks into the gravel once they landed. Driver shut off the chain saw and acknowledged the boisterous applause of his fellow gang-members with the nod of a performer taking curtain call.

'Good job, Driver,' Snake said, straddling his bike and signalling for the others to do the same. 'Now that the Sheriff is cut off from the rest of the world, we're all set to spring Jenko!' He paused, letting his men get a few more raucous whoops out of their system, then went on, 'All right, we swing by Bernie's Cafe and meet up with the rest of the Warriors, then we'll move in and take the whole town down the sewer. We'll teach Bad Rock better than to mess with us!'

More lusty battle cries sounded above the labouring engines as the Road Warriors once more took to the asphalt. With reckless abandon, they weaved back and forth, using both lanes of the road, sometimes missing each other by mere inches. For almost a mile they drove without encountering any other traffic, then a lone station wagon made the mistake of being in the wrong place at the wrong town. A family of tourists from France were inside the vehicle, and the father was frozen with fear at the sight of the approaching horde. Pulling off to the side of the road, he quickly instructed his wife and children to roll up their windows. As they shivered with dread, the Road Warriors veered their course and slowed down as they passed along both sides of the wagon. Snake helped himself to the car's antenna, while the biker across from him ripped the side-view mirror off the vehicle. The others were content to either lash out with their boots and dent the quarterpanels or spit at the windows. Driver was the last to pass by, and he stopped his bike long enough to fire up the chainsaw and decimate one of the wagon's rear tyres. By the time they'd finished thrashing the wagon, it looked as if it had just been through the blender. While unharmed, the family inside continued to shake, even after the drone of engines had receded in the distance. When the wife found her voice, she began to weep, assuring her husband that God had wreaked vengeance upon them for playing the slot machines in Vegas.

Bernie's Cafe was located adjacent to the other truck stop serving the Bad Rock/Fair City vicinity, and was the favourite of trucker hauling illegal loads and taking the back road so they wouldn't have to hassle with weighing stations. It was also a biker's hangout, and more than a dozen other choppers were already parked in front when Snake and his troops arrived.

Construction was going on in the lot next to Bernie's and there was a bulldozer and large crane standing unattended alongside a porto-john and a few stacks of lumber.

'Hey, maybe we oughta borrow ourselves that dozer, Snake,' Driver suggested as they headed for the cafe entrance. 'We could put a few nice dents in the town with that mother.'

'Yeah, and it'd also take us half a day to drive it there,' Snake said. 'Forget it. We go in fast and light. Maybe we'll cruise over there before we head out, though, and see if they got some dynamite lyin' around.'

The Road Warriors were all inside, revelling in a reunion with the other members of the gang already holding down a few booths, when the A-Team's van came up on Bernie's Cafe from the direction of Bad Rock. Face spotted the bikes and looked over at Hannibal. 'A hundred miles, huh?'

Hannibal shrugged. 'If I was right all the time, Face, I could start a religion.'

'It'd be a lot less dangerous.' Face drove by the cafe, casting a final glance at the assembled bikes. It was a vision that gnawed on his conscience, and a few dozen yards down the road he began slowing down. 'Those creeps are on their way to break their boss outta jail,' he said, thinking aloud. 'Sheriff's gonna be dogmeat.'

'Yeah, he is, isn't he?' Hannibal said. 'You know, I've been thinking about all of this anyway.'

Face pulled off to the shoulder. 'Me too.'

'Yeah?' Hannibal asked him.

'Yeah.'

'Hey, what's goin' on up there, man?' BA shouted from the back. 'We stoppin' for a picnic or something?'

'Cool it, BA,' Hannibal said, thoughtfully toying with a fresh cigar. 'You know, Face, it isn't right to lock up someone in their own jail. It's fun, but it isn't right. Heck, he never really did anything wrong.'

'Yeah, the poor guy was just doing his job.' Face prepared to crank the steering wheel hard to the left. 'So do we turn around?'

'If we want to make my momma proud, we have to,' Hannibal said.

'What about the military police?'

Hannibal thought it over as he fired up his cigar. As he shook out his match and set it in the ashtray, he said, 'You know, there's an old Indian saying, Face. Goes something like this: "When you're in water over your head, swim like hell."'

BA was listening, and he bellowed, 'Man, what's that got to do with anything?'

'Who knows?' Hannibal admitted. 'At any rate, it's time we got creative. Face, let's do an about-face and pull into that construction site back next to that cafe. I'll flag down Murdock.' He grabbed the radio microphone to broadcast the updated news to the sedan. 'I'm afraid it's showtime all ready, guys and dolls. We've got a one-act play without a curtain and, please, no smoking in the theatre.'

By the time the van had backtracked to the construction site, the sedan was already on the scene and Murdock pulled off the road to join the others. Before getting out of the van, Hannibal handed BA a revolver. 'Sorry you have to sit this dance out, big guy, but here's a little something in case one of those dirtballs comes over and gets fresh.'

'I can handle it, man.'

'Good.' Hannibal got out of the van just as Amy and Murdock were coming over. 'Amy, you stay with BA. Murdock, do you think you can fire that crane up and drive it over to the side of the cafe over there?'

'Hey, if it's got wings I can fly it,' Murdock said.

'Murdock...'

'No problem, Colonel,' Murdock said, snapping off a salute and wandering off to the hulking piece of machinery.

'Face, go and grab up a couple of those rolls of cable over by the lumber.'

'Sure thing, Hannibal,' Face said, grinning with anticipation. 'Oh, I can see this is going to be good...'

'What are we doing?' Amy wondered.

Hannibal gestured over to the cafe, where a few of the parked motorcycles were visible from the construction site. 'Gonna slow the Road Warriors down a couple hours so we can go back and help the Sheriff dig in for the attack.'

'But aren't the military police on their way?'

Hannibal smirked, puffing a cloud of smoke as he arched his eyebrows. 'Exciting, isn't it?'

TWENTY-EIGHT

Crawling on their bellies through the dirt, Hannibal and Face moved from bike to bike, threading the thick steel cable through each rear wheel they came to. Once they had a whole row of the choppers linked, Hannibal fed out more cable and Face slithered back to where they'd begun their dastardly enterprise, forming a large loop. Using an industrial-sized clip, he joined the end of the cable to the point where it passed through the first cycle, then winked at Hannibal and gave him a thumbs up. Hannibal crawled away from the bike rack, then rose to his feet and wiped the dirt from his chest as he glanced past their handiwork at Murdock, who was in the cockpit of the relocated crane, looking like some modern-day Jonah in the belly of a metallic dinosaur. Hannibal passed along the thumbs up signal to Murdock, then took a deep breath and moved around the exterior of the cafe until he came upon a large picture window overlooking the main road.

On the other side of the window, the Road Warriors were in mid-meal, psyching each other up for their coming exploits and terrorizing the waitresses in the process. Bottles of beer littered the table where Snake held court with senior members of the gang, and most of them were empty.

'And you shoulda seen the look on the lady's face when I grabbed the antenna!' Snake was boasting. 'I'll bet ya she had kittens, a whole litter of 'em, right there on the spot. Funniest damn thing I ever saw!'

'The old man was a crack-up, too!' Driver put in, reaching for his beer. 'He was sittin' behind the window lookin' like John Wayne until I ripped off the mirror, then he started turnin' yellow!'

'And green!' Snake laughed. 'Boy, were his kids gonna –'

Snake was interrupted by a sudden tapping on the window next to him. He turned around and saw Hannibal staring in at him.

'Ah, excuse me,' Hannibal said, raising his voice to be heard through the glass. 'But haven't we met before?'

'You!' Snake sneered. 'Hey, fella, we're out a couple of our bikes on account of you. Not too smart of you showin' your face here unless you're thinkin' of replacin' 'em.'

'Well, not exactly,' Hannibal taunted coyly. 'As a matter of fact, I just wanted to point out that you guys are illegally parked outside here with the bikes you still have.'

'Oh, that's real rich, man,' Snake laughed. 'You're a laugh a minute...'

'But I'm not joking, boys,' Hannibal replied calmly. 'State regulations are you gotta park your bikes at least sixteen feet inside the kerb. Most of you aren't even close. Look, I'm tryin' to be a nice guy, here; give you a little privileged info. Now, if you don't want to take it, well –'

'I'm gonna blink, ace, and when I open my eyes I want to see you gone,' Snake threatened, pointing his beer bottle at Hannibal as if it were a mortar launcher. 'Understood?'

Hannibal sighed and took a step back from the window, exclaiming, 'On the other hand, fellas, don't bother to get up on my account. I'll move 'em myself.' Spinning around, Hannibal waved to Murdock and shouted, 'Okay, hit it!'

Howling Mad Murdock started grinding gears and shifting levers, guiding the towering crane through its slow, lumbering motions. The girded neck of the crane reached upward, and Murdock simultaneously began reeling in the excess cable. The line gradually drew taut and the loop around the parked bikes slowly tightened as well. One by one, the bikes shifted, their rear tyres drawing closer together. Some tipped over and were dragged across the ground, until at last there was no slack left and the crane began hauling the cluster of bikes up into the air like a string of fish being put on display for pictures at some seaside bait shop.

'What the hell is this!' Snake screeched, staring bug-eyed at the exhibition taking place outside the window. In his hurry to bolt out of his booth, he became tangled with his fellow bikers, who were all simultaneously trying to get outside.

Face had already raced across the street and hopped into the van. Amy had left the engine running, and she slipped into the back of the vehicle as Face took over behind the wheel and squealed across the street, pulling up alongside Hannibal as he was fleeing the cafe parking lot. Hannibal opened the passenger's door and climbed up into the seat as Face sped off, giving a few toots of the horn before waving to Murdock. Still inside the cockpit of the crane, Murdock hurriedly unscrewed the lever operating the main controls and stuck it in his pocket as he ripped the ignition wires loose, shutting down the engine. He jumped down from the cockpit and broke into a frenzied run towards the fleeing van. Behind him, the first of the bikers were charging out of the cafe and gawking at the choppers that were still suspended in the air above the parking lot. One of them jerked out a pistol and started firing. Bullets skimmed across the gravel near Murdock's feet as he pumped his arms furiously, picking up enough speed to reach the rear of the van, where Amy had opened the doors and was reaching out for him. BA was holding onto Amy, allowing her to concentrate on helping pull Murdock aboard.

'All p... present and accounted for!' Murdock chimed breathlessly, collapsing to the carpeted floor of the van as Face slammed down on the accelerator and outran the next volley of bullets. Hannibal rolled down his window and stuck his head out, enjoying his last glimpse of the crane and its dangling booty.

'That ought to hold 'em off for a couple hours, huh?' he said, pulling his head back in and grinning back at those in the rear of the van. 'Nice job, Murdock. How'd you learn to operate a crane like that?'

'State fair,' Murdock said, mimicking the reeling of a miniaturized arcade steam shovel. 'Man, I won myself so many of them palm-sized cameras I could have been a distributor!' Sitting up across from BA, he smiled at the wounded man and asked, 'How's my blood brother doing?'

'I ain't your blood brother,' BA said coldly, shifting on the gurney so he wouldn't have to look at Murdock. He didn't have as much luck tuning his banter out, though.

'Sure you are, bro,' Murdock maintained. 'You have Howlin' Mad in your veins now, kid. Wait until the clouds catch fire... it's like the Fourth of July. My, my...'

As Murdock savoured the image, BA appealed to the front seat. 'Hannibal, make this sucker shut up. If I could get up, I'd plough him under, man. Take care of him even before Face if he doesn't shut up!'

'Now, now, bro,' Murdock scolded. 'Talk like that's gonna put you in the room with the rubber walls. It's no fun there...'

'Murdock, shut up or I'm gonna put you in the box with no windows!' BA struggled to get out of the gurney, but Amy rushed over and held him down.

'BA, Murdock, stop it, the both of you!' she demanded. 'Honestly, you're like five year olds sometimes.'

'You heard the lady,' Hannibal called back. 'We still have our work cut out for us, so let's put the intramural fencing on hold for the time being, okay?'

Murdock and BA both lapsed into sullen silence as Face cruised along the road leading back into Bad Rock. 'So what's our plan of attack gonna be, Hannibal?' he asked. 'The jail, huh?'

Hannibal nodded. 'The Sheriff's gonna be real hard to deal with. They get kinda testy when you lock 'em up in their own jails. I mean, look at our buddy Colonel Lynch. Ten years and he's still sore...'

'Yeah.' Face looked in the rear view mirror, catching Amy's eye. 'Well, Amy'll smile at him, right, kid? Get his heart thawed out for us.'

Amy blinked and cocked her head to one side, making a face. 'Amy will what?'

'We all use what we got, kid,' Hannibal said.

'Can we cut the kid crap, guys?' Amy snapped. 'Look, once we get to town, I'll give you your smile, then I'm going to track down Simon and work on my story. I don't need this kind of abuse.'

Face sniffed the air, then put on a British accent and told Hannibal, 'I smell mutiny in the air, Captain Bligh.'

Hannibal sniffed, too, then shook his head. 'No, lad, it's a mere tempest brewing up out to sea. We'll steer our course away from it till she calms down.'

Both men stole glances back at Amy, at the same time offering up conciliatory smiles.

'That's it, boys, lay on the charm and all fences will be mended, right?' Amy said. 'With grins like that, why do you need me? Handle the Sheriff yourselves.'

'Okay, look, Amy,' Hannibal apologized. 'I'm sorry. It's just that a team like ours is made up of folks with different specialties. I'd go in drag if I thought I could get a little mileage in the womanly charm department, but I don't have the legs for it. Do you understand? You're a vital part in our unit as long as you fill your function. It's got nothing to do with being sexist.'

'All right, all right.' Amy crossed her arms and sat back next to Murdock. 'Charges dropped ... for the time being.'

'Thank you. Now then ...' They were just coming into town, and Hannibal turned his attention to the storefronts lining main street. He pointed and said, 'Face, take a look up there. That hardware store could double nicely. We could work a shell game on those geeks when they roll in.'

'Could work,' Face said, taking in the building. 'We're dealing with double digit I.Q.s, after all. But it's gonna take time, Hannibal. MPs are on the way, too, remember. I give us two hours, three max ...'

'No sweat. It's just a basic set-dressing problem. In the movies we do it all the time. Nothing to it.'

'Worth a try.'

In the back, Murdock was getting restless. In a soft voice, he began singing to himself, 'He ain't heavy, he's my brother.'

'I ain't your brother!' BA roared. 'Hannibal, I'm tellin' ya, I had enough of this!'

Hannibal ignored the squabbling this time. Face pulled up in front of the jail and stopped, announcing, 'Here we are.'

'Okay, everybody out but Amy,' Hannibal said.

'What?' Amy said.

'Before you go to track down Simon, could you run out to Doc Sullivan's and let her out of the closet?' Hannibal asked. 'We might be needing her again before this is all over. See if she has a wheelchair she can bring for BA, too.'

'I thought I was supposed to charm the Sheriff,' she said sarcastically, moving up to the front seat as Face stepped out of the van.

'We gotta cool him down first,' he explained.

'How you doin', BA?' Hannibal said, noticing the wounded man sitting up in the gurney. 'You able to get around a litle on your own till Amy gets you a go-cart?'

'I think so,' BA said, struggling to his feet. He didn't look too stable, though. 'Might need a little help.'

'He ain't heavy...' Murdock began singing again as he moved over to assist BA, who promptly swatted his helping hand away.

'No way, sucker! Hannibal...'

Hannibal got out and moved around to help BA climb down to the street. After Amy drove off in the van, Murdock led the way into the jail, where Sheriff Thompson and Deputy Harmson were still held captive in the cell that had briefly held Face and Hannibal. Jenko was back on his cot, dozing fitfully.

'You came back,' Thompson said, spotting Hannibal and Face.

'That's right,' Hannibal said, easing BA into the swivel chair behind Harmon's desk before approaching the cell.

'Okay, I'll bite,' the sheriff ventured. 'Why?'

'You were supposed to count to a hundred and yell "Here I come, ready or not."' Face told him. 'We didn't hear you. If you're not gonna play the game, Sheriff, then we're just gonna pack up and go play somewhere else.'

'That's very funny,' Thompson responded coolly. 'You'll

forgive me if I don't break down laughing.'

'Yeah, that's the funny part, all right,' Hannibal said. 'Here's the unfunny part... there's a few dozen Road Warriors about ten miles north of here. We slowed 'em down for a couple hours, but sooner or later they're gonna show up, and it won't be to sell Girl Scout cookies.' He looked over at Jenko, who was awake now and listening in. 'They're looking to make a garbage run; pick up this piece of trash and bust up the whole town for good measure.'

'Hey, now we're cookin'!' Jenko enthused, rising from his cot and strolling over to the bars. 'Now things is lookin' right. Hey, Sheriff, you ever seen what happens when the Warriors make a run? It's beautiful. But we're real hard on cops and civilized women.'

Hannibal pulled out one of the service revolvers he'd borrowed from Thompson and cocked the hammer as he drew aim on Jenko's face. 'Hey, fat mouth, before you start jumping up and clicking your heels, let me remind you that I've got no problem just blowin' you away, right here. I'm not a cop. I'm a fugitive, just like yourself, and every now and then I like to drop the hammer on a piece of dirt like you, just to keep me in practice.'

Jenko backed away from the bars, murmuring, 'You're nuts.'

'Far from it, chump,' Hannibal said. 'I just happen to have a grudge against your family tree. You were askin' how we knew about your brother, remember? Well, we put the finger on him for his little potshot parties with some of the other SWAT boys. He gave me a hard time and now he's in traction, staring at life without parole. He got off easy compared to what's in store for you if you don't shut up and stay shut up until this is over. Do I make myself clear, or maybe you want to test me and see if I'm just nuts?'

As Jenko was digesting Hannibal's revelation, Murdock fluttered over to the cell and started batting eyelashes at the prisoner inside.

'What's his story?' Jenko said nervously, retreating to his cot.

'I'm the blood lady,' Murdock cooed. 'I give blood to guys

with holes in them. Perhaps we could do some business, muchacho. I have this feeling you're going to be leaking from three or four holes in a minute. Our rates are low. Twenty dollars a pint. We're having a special if you buy in bulk...'

Unnerved, Jenko slumped to the cot and turned his back to his tormentors. Hannibal lowered the gun and moved back over to the other cell, lowering his voice for a private conversation with Sheriff Thompson. 'Here's the new game plan... it's a combination of hide-and-seek and Red Rover, Red Rover, will the Sheriff come over.' When Thompson frowned with confusion, Hannibal spelled it out more simply. 'We let you out and we help you chase off this biker gang.'

Thompson tried taking a hard negotiating line. 'If you let me out,' he said, 'what's to stop me from calling up the National Guard and bustin' the whole bunch of you?'

'That one's easy.' Hannibal took a few steps backward and picked up one of the phones. 'Hear any dial tone?'

'I can't hear anything from this far away.'

'Well, take my word for it, Sheriff. The line's dead. The Road Warriors cut the phone lines down... and the radio in our van, which isn't here anyway, can't transmit through the mountains between here and Fair City.'

'Meaning what?'

'Meaning we're all kinda in the same corner,' Hannibal stated.

'You read the printout on us,' Face told Thompson. 'We were a commando team in Nam. We're weapons and tactics experts. We enjoy a challenge. And on top of that our prices are high and it's a heck of a living.'

Thompson looked over at his deputy for another opinion, but Harmson seemed only befuddled by the situation. After taking a deep breath, the sheriff asked Hannibal, 'How long do we have?'

'Like I mentioned before,' Hannibal replied, 'You could say we hung 'em up for a couple hours.'

Thompson crossed his arms and walked a few tight circles around the cell, deliberating. He finally stopped and shook his head. 'I can't make a deal with wanted men. I can't agree to let fugitives protect this town. I'm a police officer.'

Murdock raised an imaginary violin to his chin and began playing it with sweeps of an equally imaginary bow.

'If I were you, Sheriff,' Hannibal recommended, 'I wouldn't stand around and debate technicalities.'

Thompson hesitated again, but Harmson by now had pretty much put things into focus. 'We could die, Sheriff. Those Warriors're killers. We're locked up in here.'

'Well done, Harmson,' Face said.

Thompson relented, but glared at Hannibal as he did so, complaining, 'I suppose you want to get paid?'

'That would be nice,' Hannibal admitted. 'But, to be perfectly honest with you, Sheriff, we'd probably do this one for fun.'

'Okay, okay. You're on,' Thompson said. 'Let me out.'

Face grabbed the keys and went to unlock the cell door, but Hannibal motioned for him to wait. 'Not so fast,' he said. 'Sheriff, I want your handshake that you're not going to pull down on us with your badge and gun if we let you out. Same goes for your deputy.'

'A handshake isn't exactly a binding document,' Thompson said.

When you live on the edge,' Hannibal countered, 'you learn to make accurate evaluations of people. Your life depends on it. My take on you is that your handshake is your word. I could be wrong, but indulge me.'

Hannibal put his hand out through the bars and stared at Thompson. The sheriff uncrossed his arms and shook hands with Hannibal.

'Thanks,' Hannibal murmured as Face unlocked the cell. 'I needed that...'

TWENTY-NINE

'Typical! It's just typical. I should have known!' Amy muttered, heading back for the van, which was parked in front of the Red Rock Travel Lodge on Main Street. She'd stopped by on the way to Dr Sullivan's in hopes of catching Simon Commonble, only to discover that he'd checked out an hour before, saying he was in a hurry to catch a plane to Los Angeles to meet with her. Getting back behind the wheel, she let out a short, bitter laugh. 'Oh well, that's the high price of the jazz...'

Driving out to Dr Sullivan's residence, she parked and went inside. The doctor was still pounding on the closet door, crying for help.

'Okay, relax, Doc, I'm here.' Amy unlocked the door and let Sullivan out.

'Well, thank you for nothing!' the doctor said icily.

'Sorry, but that's the way it had to be.'

'It's inexcusable,' Sullivan huffed, 'I don't care what the situation is!' She marched over to the phone, then quickly remembered that Hannibal had ripped the cord out.

'Don't bother trying another one,' Amy said as Sullivan headed for the kitchen. 'The Road Warriors cut all phone lines into Bad Rock.'

'What?'

'You heard me. They're out at a place called Bernie's Cafe, ready to come in here and burn this town down. Now, you can bad mouth my friends all you want, but they're down at

169

the jail right this moment, helping the Sheriff get ready to defend the town. They didn't have to do that. Considering the reception they've gotten here, they would have been within their rights just driving off and leaving Bad Rock to the dogs. So you spent an hour in a closet. Big deal...'

Dr Sullivan dropped into a chair and let out a sigh, putting things into a new perspective. Looking over at Amy, she said, 'Okay, you're right. But if you would have seen the moves Hannibal put on me before shoving me in the closet, you'd know why I'm upset.'

'You're probably right on that count,' Amy admitted. 'There's a lot of old school in him when it comes to dealing with women. The bottom line, though, is that he's always got a reason for seeming to be such a creep I figure I'll get used to his style one of these decades.'

The women shared a few quick laughs, then Sullivan stood up and said, 'Okay, what's our next move? I want to help.'

'Good.' Amy went over to the far wall, where a wheel-chair was folded up and propped against a filing cabinet. She went over and unlocked its wheels, then rolled it toward the door. telling Sullivan, 'Let's take this and whatever supplies you might think we could use. There's a first aid kit in the van, but we don't have all we need. I hope it won't come to it, but I think we ought to be ready for gunplay.'

Sullivan nodded stiffly as she loaded surgical tools into a large satchel already half-filled with other medical supplies. Amy helped her lift it into the wheelchair, then they left the house and transferred the wares to the back of the van.

'How's my patient?' Sullivan asked as they got inside.

Amy backed out of the driveway, then started back into town. 'BA? Better... he's started growling again.'

As they passed through the last few acres of open space between her home and Bad Rock, Sullivan gazed out the window and smiled sardonically. 'Road Warriors, huh? Well, that ought to pick up the pace around here.'

'Couple days in a row of it.'

'I know,' Sullivan said. 'I just hope it doesn't go down as one of the darker days in Black Rock.'

'It won't if the A-Team has anything to say about it.'

'The A-Team?'

'That's what Hannibal and the others call themselves.'

'Any idea why?'

'You know, come to think of it, I don't,' Amy confessed. 'Easy to remember, I guess.'

'They're certainly an odd lot, I have to say.'

'Yeah, but the more you get to know them, the more you like them. They're genuine... real characters.'

'How'd you tie up with them anyway?' Mo asked.

'It's a long story,' Amy answered evasively, relieved to see that they were back in town. She pulled up to the sheriff's office, telling the doctor, 'Maybe I'll tell you about it some time.'

Thompson and Harmson were already out of the cell when Amy and Mo entered the jailhouse. BA was writing out a list at the desk while the other men milled around the centre of the room, discussing strategy. Spotting Sullivan, Hannibal remarked, ''lo, Doc. No hard feelings, I hope.'

'You owe me dinner when this is over,' she answered, smirking slightly before turning to Thompson. 'Hank, is this really happening?'

Thompson nodded bleakly. 'Near as I can figure, we're going to have our hands full in an hour or two.'

Harmson said, 'I think our first move should be to get Jenko outta here. Let me haul him out to Fair City.'

'You'd be wading through Warriors before you got there,' Hannibal countered. 'I'm for the home court advantage. There's no need to move Jenko. All we gotta do is put a sock in his mouth.'

'Not move him?' Harmson said, 'I don't know about that. I mean, I see your point and all, but they're just gonna roll in here and shoot up this jail if he's –'

'No, they're not,' Hannibal corrected. 'They're gonna shoot up that vacant real estate office on the east end of town.'

'How's that?' Thompson said. 'Why would they do something like that?'

'Because that's where they're gonna think the jail is,'

Hannibal said. He looked over at Harmson's desk. 'Hey, BA, how you coming along with the logistics?'

BA held up the list. Face went over to get it. 'Most of the stuff'll be easy to get, 'cept for the speakers,' BA explained. 'They gotta be good ones. Can't have no woof or wow. Gotta sound real good.'

'I'll do the best I can,' Face promised.

'That's not good enough,' Murdock said, moving over towards the desk. 'Hey, when my blood brother asks for something, Face, he –'

BA cleared his throat menacingly, shutting Murdock up. As Face left the jail to track down supplies, BA pointed to the wheelchair Amy had rolled in and said, 'Hannibal, I wanna be real close on the mechanical stuff. Someone's gonna have to wheel me around.'

Hannibal and BA simultaneously shifted their gazes to Murdock.

'Hey, I'm a pilot, not a nurse's aide!' Murdock protested. 'I respectfully refuse on the grounds that I ain't strong enough to wheel this big, ugly mudsucker around. Besides, I've lost blood. I feel faint.'

BA leaned across the desk and clamped a hand around Murdock's wrist, wheeling him around. 'Do it or I take the rest of your blood the hard way.'

'On the other hand,' Murdock chuckled uneasily. 'Blood's thicker than water, right, bro?'

'I ain't your bro, fool!'

'Okay, listen up!' Hannibal said, cutting short the altercation. Once he had everyone's attention, he laid out the battle plan. 'That abandoned real estate office offers the best tactical advantage for us. It's on the far end of town. There's a straight line of fire from the church's steeple. We're gonna draw those grizzlies out there, turn 'em around and force 'em to run a very special gauntlet. We haven't got much time, so let's get to it . . .'

THIRTY

George Tiebert was the proprietor of the Bad Rock General Store. Grey-haired, lean, and myopic, he had the demeanor of the genial shopkeeper in television commercials that the whole town relies upon to see that those with dandruff, halitosis, and haemorrhoids are taken aside for some friendly advice and sent on their way with this week's miracle cure. He was somewhat astonished that Sheriff Thompson would drop by seeking a few products to aid in the control of biker attacks.

'I don't understand,' George said, scratching his head, which was flake-free – he scratched it the way Aladdin rubbed lamps; to summon forth assistance from the forces trapped within. 'A motorcycle gang, you say?'

'Yes, George,' Thompson said patiently. 'The whole town's been talking about it all day. Surely you've heard.'

'Can't say as I have,' George confessed, eyeing Murdock and BA with consternation. 'Truth is, I just got into work a few minutes ago. Fish was bitin' real good up to Olmstead Lake, so I just stayed there till I ran outta bait –'

'That's great, George, really,' Thompson said, motioning behind his back for BA to keep his temper in check, 'but the fact of the matter is, we're a little pressed for time. You see, I've got this fella over in the jail, and he's the leader of this bike gang. They're coming back to try and bust him outta town. We want to stop 'em, and we need your help.'

'Well, I sure am flattered, Hank,' George said, 'but it's

been a while since my army days, and my back's nowhere near what it used to be. Listen, maybe you should call –'

'I can't call anywhere, George! The phones are dead,' Thompson told him. 'Those guys knocked down the lines. They mean business. So, like I say, we're going to need some of your hardware supplies. Then I want you to get to everybody in town. Tell 'em what's going on. Tell 'em we could use some help, but to get the women and children in their cars and send 'em outta town, going south. Deputy Harmson's already getting word around to folks on the east side of the street. Can I count on you for the west?'

George straightened his posture, visibly rising to the occasion. Taking off his work apron, he gave a mock salute and told Thompson, 'You sure can, Sheriff. I'll get right on it. And help yourselves to whatever you need. We'll show those hooligans a thing or two, right?'

'Right, George. Thanks a lot.'

Once Tiebert was out the door, Thompson told BA and Murdock, 'If you can handle things here, I'd just as soon get back to the jail. I don't want to leave Jenko untended any longer than I have to.'

'Sure thing, Sheriff,' Murdock said. 'Us brothers work well as a team. We'll get the job done.'

BA waited until Thompson had left, then glared over his shoulder. 'I'm not going to warn you again, sucker!'

'Okay, okay, BA . . .'

'Now you're rhymin' again, fool!' BA said. 'Shut up and push me back into the warehouse so we can get what we need and get outta here!'

Murdock glumly took up position behind BA and wheeled him through the archway leading to the back warehouse, a storage room twice the size of the main storefront.

'Turn right,' BA ordered.

Murdock swung the chair down the first aisle, complaining, 'Can't I just turn into a pumpkin? This is no fun. BA, I can't stand this sibling rivalry!'

'Shut up, you crazy fool!' BA pulled his list from his shirt pocket. 'Now, get hoppin'. First off, we need some audio wire, then a pole and some kinda stand...'

'Hey, one thing at a time!' Murdock said as he tracked down the requested supplies, working up a quick sweat. 'I haven't been hassled like this since I was a stock boy at A & P back in high school... Hey, BA, you got an uncle who lives in Oklahoma City by any chance?'

'Just keep getting them supplies, Murdock. Gonna need that metal plate over there... better, yet, get two of 'em!'

'I just love this guy!' Murdock hissed under his breath as he started loading things into a shopping cart.

'Come on, sucker, we ain't got no time for your crazy rap!'

Once Murdock picked up his momentum, it only took a few more minutes to track down the other materials BA had decided were needed to wage their defence of Bad Rock. They had two filled shopping carts when they were through, and Murdock butted them, one in front of the other, so that BA could push them while he was pushing BA, allowing them to pass through the huge doors of the loading dock in one trip.

'I'm a caboose and I'm on the looooooose!' Murdock sang as their motley caravan neared the A-Team van parked next to the dock.

'You got somethin' loose, all right,' BA told him. 'I'm a lucky guy if I don't catch your craziness. Now get down and I'll pass this stuff to you so you can load it in the van. I don't gotta get outta my chair to handle that.'

Shifting the supplies from the carts took another few minutes, then BA wheeled himself down a ramp leading to the parking lot. The effort exhausted him, and he was gasping for breath when Murdock came over, lapsing into a rare moment of seriousness.

'Okay, partner, no more fun and games. Here, let me help you up into the van.'

'Thanks, Murdock,' BA wheezed, slowly rising from his chair. Murdock put an arm around him and helped guide him up into the passenger's seat. 'You're okay when you ain't tryin' to make me crazy.'

'Just doin' what comes natural,' Murdock said. 'C'mon, let's see what the rest of the crew is up to...'

Down at the other end of the block, Hannibal and Face were securing bars into place in the front window frames of the real estate office while Amy and Mo Sullivan straddled ladders and hammered a whitewashed panel of plyboard over the sign proclaiming the profession of the building's former tenants. As Murdock pulled up in front, BA rolled down his window and called out, 'Got everything we need, Hannibal. Now we just gotta set it all up.'

'Consider it done,' Hannibal said. 'Mo, Amy, Face... why don't you unload this stuff while Murdock climbs up and paints us a new sign...'

'Me?' Murdock said.

'That's right, Murdock. I've seen the job you've done on some of the walls in your rooms back at the VA, and you're definitely the man for the job.'

'Why, I'm flattered, Colonel,' Murdock said. 'What should I write? How about "Bad Rock Institute of Corrective Incarceration"? No, too long. How about "Penal Quarters –"'

'How about "Jail", Murdock?'

'Right,' Murdock said, accepting the bucket of paint and brush Hannibal held out to him. Assuming the dainty airs of an interior decorator, he gushed, 'I think that would capture the ambiance just perfectly!'

As Murdock started up the ladder, he paused and sniffed the rim of the bucket, then dabbed his finger in the paint and sampled it like a master chef testing sauce. 'Mmmmm, not bad. Good body, fine bouquet. Nice vintage indeed!'

Hannibal looked over at the van, where BA was staring at Murdock with disbelief. 'BA, you haven't started rhyming words, have you?'

'Nope.'

'Good.'

In the back of the van, Amy and Mo were withdrawing two of the bulky metal sheets that had been procured from the general store. Amy asked Face, 'What are we going to do with these?'

'Hot plates,' Face said. 'They make great hot plates.'

'Hot plates?'

'Yeah... we're having Warrior burgers for supper.'

THIRTY-ONE

When informed of the impending arrival of the Road
Warriors, the overwhelming majority of Bad Rock residents
opted for various forms of strategic retreat rather than
volunteering to aid in the town's defence. Some packed
overnight bags and headed south, determined to stay away
from the envisioned carnage until the smoke and rubble had
settled. Others loaded up on rations and fled to the old
Presbyterian Church outside of town, figuring that they
could find safety in numbers and at the same time have a
more direct access to the heavenly switchboard when they
prayed for deliverance from the hands of the infidels, both
those approaching Bad Rock and those who had struck up
an unholy alliance with Sheriff Thompson. Some vowed to
fight back against the intruders, but chose to limit their
battlelines to the borders of their property. Many a
homeowner peered out through drawn shades, awaiting the
first sign of trespass, armed with anything from shotguns to
rolling pins. In all, the recruitment drive waged by Deputy
Harmson and George Tiebert netted four residents willing to
work along with the A-Team, and those four remained only
long enough to help with the final touches on the refurbished
real estate office or the bonafide jail, which was made over to
look like it contained property listings rather than the
scruffy degenerate who was responsible for the entire
commotion. Harmson spelled Thompson at the jail, and
Hank ambled down the middle of the deserted street like

Gary Cooper in *High Noon*, approaching the other building, where there was still a bustling of activity.

'It's been almost an hour and a half,' he said to Face, who was overseeing Murdock's painting of the sign over the doorway. 'If they're coming, it won't be long now...'

'Almost ready, Sheriff.'

'Where's Hannibal?'

'Inside, rigging up the sound system.'

Thompson nodded greetings to Amy and Mo Sullivan, who were reinforcing the putty that held the window's bars in place, then opened the door and walked into the building. The interior was little more than a vacant shell, save for the centre of the main room, where Hannibal was hooking up a pair of expensive-looking speakers to a large amplifier.

'Ah, you're just in time, Sheriff,' Hannibal told him, plugging a microphone into the amplifier. Speaking into it, he said, 'Testing, one, two, three... how's that coming through, BA?'

From out in the street, BA shouted, 'Turn it down just a little, Hannibal.'

Hannibal made the appropriate adjustment, then began uncoiling the long length of wire connecting the mike to the amplifier. As he passed by the sheriff, feeding out more line, he said, 'We already measured this out so it'll reach all the way to your office. Talk from there and it'll sound like you're here.'

'I gotta hand it to you guys. You're fast and efficient.'

'If we weren't, we'd be dead twelve times over.' Hannibal set the mike down momentarily as he inspected the light switch next to the door. The plate was off the switch and the wires were exposed. 'Okay, ready on that front, too... Face! Where's that sign for inside here?'

Face opened the door and handed Hannibal a hand-painted sign. 'Pretty, huh? Collaboration between BA and Murdock. BA dictated and Murdock spelled it out.'

'I could have guessed that,' Hannibal said, reading the sign along with Sheriff Thompson. The sign read:

DANGER – FIVE THOUSAND VOLTS
TOUCH THIS AND YOU'RE DEAD, SUCKER

'Five thousand?' Thompson questioned. 'There's only a one ten line running into here.'

'Packaging is everything, Sheriff,' Hannibal said.

Face grabbed a wrench and screwdriver, telling Hannibal, 'I'll rig this baby up so you can run that line across the street. Showtime's almost on us.'

'Deal.'

Sheriff Thompson followed alongside Hannibal as he continued to feed out the microphone line, exiting from the building to the street. Fate's contribution to the A-Team's grand ploy had been to have this be the year Bad Rock was repaving Main Street. As such, the road was nothing but dirt, and it was relatively easy for Hannibal to cover traces of the wire. Thompson helped speed things up by taking over the concealment chores, freeing Hannibal to unwind his coil faster.

Murdock and BA were still in the middle of the street, and as he backed up alongside of them, Hannibal said, 'It's about time you two took up your position, BA, isn't it?'

'Yup,' Murdock said, starting to wheel BA away. 'Let's go steeple-chasing, my friend... notice that I call you friend instead of brother.'

'What do you want, a medal?' BA groused.

'Once you get him up there, Murdock, I want you back here for the wrap up,' Hannibal called out to the retreating twosome.

'You got it, Colonel.'

Hannibal's measurement of the microphone wire had been accurate, as it managed to reach all the way to the inside of the real jail. Standing before the window looking out on Main Street, Hannibal held the mike out to Thompson. 'Got anything to say, Sheriff?'

Thompson shook his head.

'Okay, then...' Hannibal turned on the microphone and spoke into it so that his voice was transmitted through the speakers inside the real estate office across the street. 'Amy, we're ready for that toilet paper now!'

'Toilet paper?' Thompson said, confused. 'Where does that come in?'

'If you don't know, Sheriff, I'd hate to do your laundry.'
Hannibal laughed and headed for the door. 'Just kidding.
Come on, I'll show you.'

As the two men were headed for the door, Jenko let out a
muffled roar in his cell, trying to heap profanities on the men
through his gag.

'Didn't anyone ever teach you not to talk with your mouth
full, Jenko?' Hannibal quipped on his way out the door.
'Harmson, if he does that again, send him to his cot without
supper.'

'It'd be my pleasure, believe me,' Harmson said, looking
up from the gun rack, where he was loading charges into the
riot guns.

Outside, Hannibal and Thompson crossed the street once
more, reaching the van just as Amy was pulling out an arm-
load of toilet paper.

'Okay, I give up,' Thompson said. 'What's it for?'

Hannibal grabbed one of the rolls and tossed it in the air,
then caught it. 'We're going to detour an access road with it,
what else?'

'Say what?'

'If you can ignore the obvious, Sheriff, you can do just
about anything,' Hannibal replied. 'You can quote me on
that if you want.'

'If I knew what you were talking about, I might.'

Face emerged from the redressed building just as
Murdock was jogging over from the Lutheran Church down
the street. The whole team, with the exception of BA,
gathered near the van.

'BA's in place, Colonel,' Murdock announced, pointing
over to the church steeple, where the wounded man could be
seen, waving a rifle to show his position. 'And if you don't
mind, I'd like to be up there with him. At a time like this one
should be with his family.'

Hannibal shook his head. 'War is hell, Captain. You have
to stay with the front guard.'

Murdock stood at attention and saluted. 'I understand,
Colonel.'

'Good. Now, you and Face take the toilet paper and wall

up the alley we were talking about earlier... maybe we can pile a couple bikers in there. Then, Face, you take up position on the roof of the hardware store. Amy, you, Doc and Sheriff Thompson come with me into the other jail... Hopefully this thing will go down before a load of MPs pull into town...'

THIRTY-TWO

The military police weren't the foremost threat to barge into Bad Rock before the A-Team had completed its preparations. After all, the two jeeps and one truck carrying the armed force deemed necessary to effectively transport the desperate likes of their intended prisoners was still a good ten miles away from the town. The Road Warriors, on the other hand, were twice as close, riding with adrenalin in their veins and hate in their hearts. As Murdock had anticipated, there was enough electrical expertise amongst the various bikers to finally piece together the stripped wiring in the crane cockpit, and a makeshift lever had been provided to enable Driver to lower the suspended bikes to the ground. More than half of the choppers had required repairs to some extent, and by the time Snake had given the orders to ride out, it was a toss-up as to whether the gang was more concerned about liberating Jenko Stark from prison or getting their hands on the A-Team for a nice, bloody bit of retribution.

'It's a slow death if we find them!' Snake screamed above the roar of engines. 'The first blow is mine!'

'I get second!' Driver howled.

One by one, the others lined up their reservations, all the while closing the distance between themselves and Bad Rock. This time there were no errant motorists for them to vent their rage on, and it built up inside them as they took partial solace in the opening of their throttles, picking up their speed and letting the wind whip past them. They were an awesome sight, terrifying in their reckless certainty as they rounded bends in the road without letting up with their speed, leaning their bikes at sharp angles so that their ankles came within mere inches of scraping the asphalt.

In Bad Rock, the streets were quiet and deserted. Except for a few scattered items heralding modern times, it might have been a ghost town from the days of the Old West, abandoned overnight by a passing plague or word that gold had been found in a riverbed miles to the south. But, secreted away in certain niches of that desolate silence, the A-Team lay waiting, and ready. BA was still in the church tower, rifle resting across his lap as he sat in the wheelchair, peering out at the dusty street. Several buildings away, Murdock was behind the wheel of the van, parked by the take-out window of the town's lone fast-food establishment. He hummed and drummed his fingers on the dashboard, but kept a careful eye and ear peeled for the first sign of invasion. Face was on the roof of George Tiebert's General Store, which afforded a view all the way down Main Street to the edge of town. He had a two-way radio close to his side, and it wasn't long before he put it to use.

'Here they come, Hannibal,' he reported. 'Sleazy Rider and his boys...'

Inside the would-be real estate office that housed the real jail, Hannibal picked up his radio and answered, 'We don't drop the hammer until we can smell their breath. Over.'

Thompson, Amy, and Harrison were all standing near Hannibal, each armed with a riot gun and staring out the window. Behind them, Mo Sullivan had cleared off the deputy's desk and set out her surgical instruments and supplies. 'So, it's time,' she said simply.

Hannibal glanced back at her. 'If our bluff falls through and they head here first, I want you behind the desk or in the back room before the bullets fly. You're the only Florence Nightingale we've got.'

Even as Sullivan was nodding, the Road Warriors were rolling into town, the sounds of their motors bounding starkly off the storefronts. Hannibal and the others braced themselves, fingers on the triggers of their guns, as the unruly procession began to slow down. The bikers were riding down the middle of the street, and as they passed by the foursome crouched near the window, they shifted course and turned the other way, lining up their choppers in front of the converted real estate office across the street.

As the Warriors killed their engines, Hannibal grinned. 'Well, they've sniffed out the bait. Now all we gotta do is make sure they bite it.'

Once silence had returned to the tension-filled air, Snake cupped his hands over his mouth, making a megaphone through which he shouted, 'We've come for our man, Jenko Stark. You let him out or we burn down this stinking town and roast marshmallows on the ashes!'

The other bikers, still straddling their metallic chargers, formed a semi-circle around the empty building, their backs turned to Hannibal and the others. Hannibal set down the two-way radio in favour of the microphone. Clicking it on, he began taunting, 'You pigs want Jenko? Then come in and get him, if you have the guts.' Across the way, his voice boomed out from the speakers. 'But I don't think animals like you can wipe the filth out of your eyes long enough to do the job. I'm here, c'mon in.'

'You sound like you want to die, pig!' Snake retorted. 'There's only two of you and thirty of us. You don't have enough gas to keep Jenko in there.'

'Talk, talk. You slobs heard me. You want him, you got him. Let's go. I want to play this game before it gets called off on account of darkness. I'm sick of you slimeballs puking into my town. Come on in and get him, dirtball!'

'Hey, wait a minute!' Snake said. 'I recognize that voice. You're the guy that strung us up a couple times already, right?'

'You got it, chump!'

'Well, that's fine and dandy, 'cause now we're gonna kill two birds with one stone.'

'You talk pretty big for a wimp that needs a wash, sonny...'

'You're gonna eat that, pig!' Snake shouted, jumping on his kick start and firing up his bike. The others did the same. 'Gonna feed you to my guys for dessert!'

Once all the choppers were running again, the Warriors began to pull away from what they thought was the sheriff's office.

'They're leaving!' Thompson gasped.

'Naw,' Hannibal assured him. 'Just getting a running start. Watch . . .'

Only a handful of the bikers ended up heading off, and they turned around once they were halfway down the street, then opened their throttles and picked up speed as they started back towards the dummy jail. The others cleared the way for them, and Snake led the way as the five racing choppers vaulted up the kerb and slammed through the front door of the building that supposedly held their captive leader. The door splintered on impact, and by the time Snake and his men regained control of their bikes, the opening behind them had been blocked by a pair of large steel plates that had swung down from the ceiling, along with the sign warning that the metal was charged with five thousand watts that were guaranteed to kill on touch, sucker. The exposed wires from the light switch were sparking off the plates, lending a hint of authenticity to the barrier.

'Hey, this ain't no sheriff's office!' one of the bikers deduced as he tried to pry his bike away from Snake's. None of them were about to test the plates.

The speakers had been toppled by the crashing bikes, but they were still working, and Hannibal's voice cackled out at them, 'We're taking you bozos down in bunches. Five down, fifteen to go . . . Okay, Murdock, you're on!'

Murdock started up the van and rolled out into the street, drawing the attention of the startled bikers, who immediately recognized the vehicle. Rolling down his window, Murdock called out innocently, 'I say, you chaps wouldn't perchance know the way to San Jose, would you?'

Driver revved up his bike and told the others, 'This one's mine. Anybody who wants leftovers can follow me!'

Murdock suddenly barked like a dog, then baited, 'Catch me if you can, lizard-breath!' Spinning the van around, Murdock eased down on the accelerator, then popped the clutch, racing off in a spurt that sent gravel spraying up at the eight Warriors who had taken off in pursuit of him. The dirtscreen gave him a few extra seconds, and he took advantage of them, speeding ahead of the bikers in the direction of the general store. As he passed the building, Murdock cut a sharp right and whisked into the alley, then swerved to one side, skidding to a stop in a tight space between the loading dock and a trash bin.

Moments later, the eight Warriors rounded the corner at full tilt. Unable to see Murdock's van at first, their view was immediately taken up by the sight of toilet paper drawn out in tight bands that stretched the whole width of the alley. As fast as they were travelling, though, they had no way of knowing the nature of the obstruction. Fearing that it was a solid white wall, Driver slammed on his brakes and brodied sideways. By the time he had ploughed through the tissue and come to a stop, the other bikers had followed his lead and collided into one another in their attempt to avoid contact with the would-be wall. As they were swearing and sorting themselves out, Face peered down from the rooftop of the general store and levelled his riot gun at them, warning, 'Anybody moves and I start leaking your blood on your bikes.' After making a quick count of his catch, Peck raised his radio and told Hannibal, 'I've got eight gift-wrapped in Charmin, here!'

'Seven left,' Hannibal responded. 'Okay, Murdock. About face.'

Murdock put the van in reverse and squealed out of the alley, almost running over four bikers who were bringing up the rear. They changed course in time to avoid a collision, then followed the van as it headed back the way it had come. Murdock drove past the real and bogus jails, luring his pursuers behind him. Once he was past the buildings, Hannibal suddenly burst out of the jail and jerked hard on the wire that had been buried in the dirt. The cord shot upward just as the four bikers were hurtling by, catching them across the shoulders with a stinging snap that forced their hands off the handlebars. All four bikes went immediately out of control, upending their riders like bucking broncos in the process.

'Three more,' Hannibal announced, strolling leisurely over to cover the downed men.

The three bikers in question had had a change of heart in the face of the fate that had befallen their cohorts. Deciding to flee the scene, they gunned their bikes down Main Street in the direction of the church. BA was ready for them, and two blasts of his shotgun were sufficient to rip through the front tyres of two of the bikes. The third bike was sideswiped by the chopper next to it, and Sheriff Thompson rushed out with Deputy Harmson to make sure that the gang members wouldn't resume their flight on foot.

'Well, by my count, that's all she wrote,' Hannibal said, obviously pleased with the results. He'd spoken too soon, though, for there came the splintering sound of Snake driving through the rear door of the fake jail and swinging out onto Main Street. No longer filled with bravado, he was now subscribing to the dictum that he who fights and runs away lives to fight another day. Instead of trying to get past BA, though, he tried riding off in the other direction, hoping to leave town the same way he'd entered. Sheriff Thompson raised his rifle and was ready to shoot at Snake when Hannibal stepped over and pushed down the barrel.

'Why'd you do that?' Thompson said angrily.

'Too easy,' Hannibal said. 'Let Murdock handle him.'

Murdock had just turned around and was heading back toward the jail. Seeing Snake coming towards him, he grinned maliciously and worked the steering wheel so that he was on a collision-course, recreating the first confrontation between the A-Team and the Road Warriors back on the bridge at the edge of town.

'And the winner of the game would holler "Chicken!"' Murdock shouted, bearing down on Snake.

Snake tried to veer to one side, but Murdock matched his move and continued to approach the biker head-on. A sudden gleam of mania came to Snake's eyes, and he decided to call Murdock's bluff, aiming his front tyre at the grill of the van.

Stepping out of the jail to see what was happening, Amy shrieked, 'They'll kill each other!'

But it wasn't to be. At the last second, Snake jerked his handlebars, pitching off to one side. He missed colliding with the van, but rammed instead into the kerb and was thrown headlong over his bike, doing a complete somersault in mid-air before landing in a display of lawn furniture set out in front of a summer goods shop. He stirred, but he wasn't going anywhere.

'None left,' Hannibal announced. 'Games over, gonzos!'

EPILOGUE

Battered and beaten, the Road Warriors were herded together into the middle of the street and surrounded by the allied forces that had seen to their undoing. Mo Sullivan tended to some of the more serious wounds, guarded as she did so by a gun-toting Deputy Harmson. From the sullen, downcast expressions on the bikers' faces, it seemed likely that the gravest injuries had been dealt to their egos.

'Nice of you boys to drop in when you did,' Thompson told them, unable to restrain a grin of satisfaction. 'We have a small band of military police on their way to Bad Rock, and they'll love the chance to rub elbows with your kind, I'm sure. You'll even get to be reunited with your ringleader. Of course, the closest you'll be coming to motorcycles for the next few years will be stamping bike plates in the state pen.'

Hannibal sauntered over to Thompson's side, indulging himself in his first cigar since the seige. 'You see, Sheriff? Sometimes you can change the reality of the situation.

'Wow! Reality!' Murdock whooped. 'What a concept!'

'Murdock, why don't you make yourself useful and help Face pull BA out of the church steeple?' Turning to Amy, Hannibal said, 'Miss Allen, would you be so kind as to fire up the van? We've got to get outta here before Lynch's goons show up.'

As Amy headed off, leaving Thompson and Hannibal alone, the sheriff said, 'Thanks, Hannibal. Bad Rock owes you a lot.'

'Maybe so, but I'm not worried about collecting. Knowing these worms will end up in the can's good enough for me right now.' Hannibal blew a ring of smoke, then resumed, 'Of course, I'm going to have to ask you to turn your back on us a second.'

Thompson nodded. 'I don't know what I'm gonna tell the MPs, though.'

'I'd lie if I were you, Sheriff.' Hannibal held out a hand. 'I appreciate you keeping your word.'

'I'd be a fool not to. Good luck to you, Hannibal.'

'Thanks.' As he strode down the street to the waiting van, Hannibal paused alongside Mo Sullivan. 'Well, Doc, here's where I ride off into the sunset. Wanna sing me a verse of "Happy Trails" before I go?'

Mo leaned forward and kissed Hannibal lightly on the cheek, whispering in his ear, 'Until we meet again...'

Hannibal grinned, dabbing his cheek. 'Keep smiling until then... but don't hold your breath. I don't make it to Bad Rock all that often.'

'I know,' Mo said. 'It was nice knowing you, though. I mean it.'

Hannibal waved to Harmson and the handful of local residents beginning to emerge from the woodwork, then climbed up into the van as Amy drove up next to him. By the time they reached the church, the rest of the team was waiting out in front. Face and Murdock were about to help BA get into the van when he waved them off and stood up, shoving the wheelchair aside, grumbling, 'Enough of that jive!'

'Well, hurry up and get inside, boys,' Hannibal said, peering into the rear view mirror. 'If we don't roll by a count of three, we're gonna have ourselves an escort we don't need.'

Just arriving in town was the parade of military police, a dozen men in all, spread out among three vehicles. Colonel Lynch, long-time nemesis of Hannibal Smith and the others, was riding shotgun in the front jeep. Seeing the Road Warriors gathered in the middle of the street, he rubbed his hands together expectantly. 'Will you take a look at that? Looks like the A-Team's expanded. Bad move on their part.

Probably what ended up foiling them.'

As they drew closer to the bikers, the driver of the jeep discerned the prisoner's faces and delivered the grim news. 'Colonel, I don't think this is the A-Team...'

Lynch was coming to the same, sudden realization, and the numbing rage welling up inside him kept him from bothering to stare past the gathering to the opposite end of the street, where the A-Team's van was on its way out of town.

Face was looking out the back windows, and he chuckled, 'You know, ol' Lynch is gonna go cuckoo when he finds out we jobbed him again.'

'The man's already running on a dim bulb,' Hannibal observed.

'I hear there's a lot of that going around,' Murdock said, edging closer to BA in the back of the van. 'Right, Bro?'

'I ain't your brother!' BA said. 'How many times I gotta tell you, fool?'

'Lighten up, BA,' Face said, moving away from the window and sitting down. 'It all worked out, didn't it? What the hell, Murdock's blood will probably even add a little colour to your life.'

'I got enough colour,' BA said, leaning forward and taking the rings off his right fingers. 'I also got some unfinished business with you, sucker!'

'Oh, BA, come on,' Face chuckled nervously. 'That's ancient history, for crying out loud!'

BA shook his head, cracking his knuckles. 'I got to do this, man. I owe you, then we're square. You gonna take it like a man?'

'Hannibal?' Face appealed.

'You're on your own, Face.'

'No, BA's the one who's gonna be on my own face,' Peck protested.

'Here it comes, sucker!' BA lashed out with his right forearm, but instead of striking Face with his fist, he contented himself with tweaking the other man's nose between his thumb and forefinger. Face, who had closed his eyes and cringed in anticipation of a kayo punch, dropped his jaw and blinked, staring with wonder at the fingers clamped around his nose.

'That's it?' he said, his voice twanging because of his blocked sinuses.

'That's it,. fool!' BA replied, pulling his hand away and starting to laugh.

'Oh, yeah, well then I have no choice but to retaliate.' Face placed his thumb on the tip of his throbbing nose and waved his fingers as he blew BA a raspberry.

Up behind the wheel, Amy heard the commotion and strained for a glimpse in the rear view mirror as she asked Hannibal, 'What's going on back there?'

Hannibal contorted his face into the features of his alter ego, Mister Lee, whose meeting with Ed Maloney had precipitated the past week of wild adventure. 'Honourable Confucious say: "A-Team that play together, stay together..."'